"Recreational sex?"

Jared's eyebrows rose. "Let's get one thing straight, sweetheart. I'm not looking for a quick lay and I'm too old to satisfy a herd of women."

"Sarge, I never said..." Heat flooded Marnie's cheeks.

Jared's gaze softened slightly. "I love watching you blush. You're an innocent at heart, know that?"

"I told you last night I'm not a virgin."

Jared frowned. "Innocence has nothing to do with how many guys there have been in your past. Damn it, Marnie, what's more important is how you felt about them."

She was uncharacteristically silent.

"Don't you understand, sweetheart, I don't care whether or not I'm *first* in line. As long as the line stops with me...."

Dear Reader,

Temptation is Harlequin's boldest, most sensuous romance series . . . a series for the 1990s! Fast-paced, humorous, adventurous, these stories are about men and women falling in love—and making the ultimate commitment.

Rebels & Rogues, our yearlong salute to the Temptation hero, ends this month with *The Soldier of Fortune*. Kelly Street has written a powerful story about a tough Vietnam vet who has to find the courage to fight for love.

I hope you have enjoyed all twelve Rebels & Rogues books—stories of men who are rough around the edges, but incredibly sexy. Men full of charm, yet ready to fight for the love of a very special woman. . . .

Beginning in January 1993, look for our magical new miniseries, Lovers & Legends—fairy tales retold Temptation-style. *The Perfect Husband* (#425) by popular Kristine Rolofson is the perfect start to this yearlong special!

Warm regards,

Birgit Davis-Todd
Senior Editor

P.S. We love to hear from our readers!

THE SOLDIER OF FORTUNE

KELLY STREET

Harlequin Books

TORONTO • NEW YORK • LONDON
AMSTERDAM • PARIS • SYDNEY • HAMBURG
STOCKHOLM • ATHENS • TOKYO • MILAN
MADRID • WARSAW • BUDAPEST • AUCKLAND

Thanks to the staff of Petaluma Paintball Supply

Published December 1992

ISBN 0-373-25521-7

THE SOLDIER OF FORTUNE

1

TRUMPETS BLARED. Flags waved and snapped, all color and rustling sound. The wind wasn't just blowing, it was blustery. It had roared out of the west into Liberty Hollow, Indiana, just in time for the annual parade.

Above the howling of wind, from somewhere amid the rushing of the throng of uniformed bodies that had taken over Main Street, a French horn pealed. The single note electrified the air. Another gust tore through the tunnel of buildings and ripped the sound to bits.

Then the skies opened.

Marnie Rainbrook lifted her face to fat drops of rain and laughed. When she and another teacher had dragged five of their teenage students into town away from the exclusive residential school where they all lived, she'd envisioned something a little different. Clear skies. Some of the homegrown hospitality for which small Midwestern towns were justly famous. Marnie had thought a glimpse into another, slower-paced world would be a pleasant antidote to the adolescent sophistication that plagued her charges. She should have remembered how quickly storms could race across the sky here on the edge of the prairie.

"Can you think of anything better than a marching band?" she sang out exuberantly.

The fourteen-year-old seated next to Marnie gave her a pitying glance. Obviously her remark, loud enough to be heard over a blast from the trombones of the first band that swung by, put her on the other side of the chasm that existed between Mark and *anybody* who thought there might be better things in life than sex, drugs and rock 'n' roll.

Like a turtle, he retracted his head into the crew neck of his T-shirt. He muttered, "Hell, no, Ms. Rainbrook. Sure can't."

Marnie swallowed a grin. Poor thing, his rampant teenage ego would bruise at kidding, so she let him enjoy his misery. She turned her attention to the boy squatting on the curb on her other side. Undersize, introspective, bespectacled. A natural butt for his classmate's jokes. He was watching the workings of the valves on the various instruments tootling by with avid interest.

Kevin was her favorite among this group of students. He had also tested as tone-deaf to an almost superhuman degree when he'd undergone the battery of examinations—physical, psychological and scholastic—that greeted every new student at The Oaks. A sinking feeling attacked the pit of Marnie's stomach. Kevin wasn't listening to the magnificently off-key rendition of a Sousa march. He wasn't even trying to stare up the pom-pom girls' flirty skirts. The other boys were certainly doing so. But Kevin, the misfit, was probably trying to figure out how to take the piccolo apart and turn it into a bazooka. If the report that had been forwarded to her by the school psychologist was correct, he had tried similar stunts before.

As swiftly as the storm had arrived it passed, spiriting away its overturned cauldron of black clouds and cold rain. A couple of World War I doughboys with sunken cheeks and grim mouths rode by on a platform in the watery sunshine.

"Quick, Kevin, how many stars on the flag that elderly man is carrying?" she asked.

Kevin's eyes narrowed and he pushed too-long dark hair off his forehead. With his other hand, he fingered the silver medallion that always hung around his neck. "Forty-eight," he said, and smiled shyly. "That's right, isn't it, Ms. Rainbrook?"

"Don't ask me." Marnie loved to tease this one. He always responded as if the ordinary give-and-take of conversation were a priceless gift. Not for the first time, she wondered what kind of idiots his scientist parents must be, to have mucked up such a nice kid. "I'm not the one with the computer for a brain."

"Yeah, we all know Kevin is teacher's pet," Chad, a stocky towhead, chanted in a singsong.

"Maybe Wizard *didn't* figure out how many stars. Not by just looking. Could be he's not such a brain. Prob'ly memorized how many states there were in—in—" another one of the boys stammered to a halt.

"1918," Marnie produced, unperturbed. It would do more harm than good to order the agitators to knock it off. Despite his success at instantaneously computing the number of stars on the flag, Kevin was already starting to wilt. His head and shoulders drooped.

From her gritty seat on the curb, Marnie leaned forward, hugging her knees, and peeked into his face. "Did you know that? That World War I ended in 1918?" It was certainly safe to ask. Kevin's almost complete lack of knowledge about anything except math and mechanics was one of the reasons he'd been incarcerated at The Oaks. It hadn't been the most important reason, of course. Kevin had slightly less talent for getting along with his peers than the average preschooler. She whispered, "Kevin? Have you ever *heard* of World War I?"

His head shook in a sullen negative.

Marnie patted a thin shoulder. "Well, now you have. Keep it in mind, there'll be a quiz later."

The others groaned. "A quiz!"

"Sure." She grinned at them. "On the parade. How many floats and which school has the majorettes with the best legs and—"

They groaned again, but the mood around her lightened. Even Kevin lifted his head and darted a few guarded squints at a high-stepping redhead with cornfed breasts which bounced without inhibitions—or, Marnie suspected, a bra.

Meow, Marnie reproved herself. Despite the confidence twenty-four years, dark blond hair and long legs gave her, it was still something of a trial to be reminded that men fixated on the convex parts of the female anatomy. Even fourteen-year-old males liked big breasts. And no amount of good muscle tone would ever make hers anything but, well, petite.

Marnie's elfin figure wasn't a thing she obsessed over. She was lucky enough to be healthy as well as attractive. In a strictly understated way, of course. She was also sensible enough to appreciate her good fortune.

However, every once in a while it occurred to Marnie that it might be nice to have a man look at her as if he would salivate if he weren't so polite. A real, grownup man, she added to herself, ruefully surveying her five underage dates. Oh, well. She'd fought to become a teacher. That didn't mean she couldn't have a few wistful fantasies.

"Kids sure don't know nothin' these days, do they?"

"I beg your pardon?" She turned a frosty glance on the woman seated in a sagging lawn chair close by.

"Kids." A hand with chipped red nail polish waved at the bare-legged youngsters lining the sidewalk. To Marnie's relief, the scarlet-tipped claws weren't pointing at Kevin. "When I was a young'un, my folks woulda whaled the tar outa me if I din't stand when the flag passed by."

Marnie could just barely remember being pulled to her feet to put her hand over her heart during parades she'd attended as a child. At some misty, not quite identifiable point, people had stopped telling her she had to do it. When her mother had died? No; the ritual seemed to have lost importance not just in her family, but everyone's.

Another contingent of veterans—World War II vintage, she judged from the surplus of jowls and paunches—passed by, and sure enough, the flag that accompanied the troop didn't cause a single person to pop up.

"Times change," she said diplomatically.

"More's the pity. Spoiled, these kids, with their MTV and their Super Nintendo. They miss out on a lot."

Now *that* Marnie could agree with. "The sad thing is they don't really know how to enjoy themselves," she said softly. "They act as if it were a sin to show enthusiasm."

The woman snorted. "Too much, too soon. If they hadda scratch in the dirt for a living, they'd value what they got."

A laugh choked out of Marnie. "You sound like a commercial for my school."

"I'll be." Mud-colored eyes peered from behind plastic-framed glasses held together with masking tape. The woman's lips moved as she read the words printed on Marnie's blazingly white T-shirt. It was similar to the ones the boys wore. "I'll be. You from that fancy Oaks place?"

"I used to be a student there. Now I'm a teacher."

The woman grabbed the metal armrests of her lawn chair and scooted it several inches away. "You? A nice lookin' little thing like you? At that reformatory?"

"It's not..." Marnie broke off. The woman had turned a burly, and very cold, shoulder toward her.

"Hey, Wizard! Let's see you make the basket!"

Marnie swallowed her indignation. At least none of the boys had heard.

Instead, predictably, four of them were ganging up on Kevin.

With a crumpled fast-food bag balled in his fist, Kevin was darting glances back and forth between a trash barrel and his classmates. An uncertain smile trembled on his mouth. Her own lips tensing, Marnie willed him to get the bag into the barrel.

With a flash of the whites of his eyes in her direction, Kevin threw. The bag fell like a rock six inches short.

"Wizard, you're pathetic," said Chad.

A whistle shrilled in the street. Chad's attention was jerked to a girls' drill team as if it had been pulled by a string. Knee-high white boots stamped. Tall hats with plumes threatened to fall from shaky foundations of frosted and moussed hair. A great deal of adolescent flesh jiggled.

Chad sighed. "I'm in love."

"Love at first sight is a myth," Marnie told him, laughing. "If it's that fast, it isn't love."

"What is it, then?"

"Ask Mr. Simpson when he finishes his dentist's appointment," she advised him dryly. David Simpson who had accompanied them to Liberty Hollow, taught biology.

She bent her head to Kevin's. In the loose division of labor among instructors at The Oaks, physical education fell into her area of expertise. "We'll work on the coordination, Kev. I'll put together a few exercises for you and we'll find the time for some one-on-one. Then we'll show these guys what you can do. Okay?"

He managed a sickly smile. "Yeah. Thanks, Ms. Rainbrook." Stiffly he unfolded to his feet and went to pick up the bag and deposit it in the barrel.

Marnie chewed her lip. No wonder she'd become fond of him in the month since he'd joined the student body for summer quarter. Along with a full course of academics and the other, less customary skills emphasized at The Oaks, the school tried to imbue respect for the environment. Kevin seemed to be getting the message.

Gulf War soldiers in modern, spanking clean uniforms clattered by. They were followed by more bands, more baton twirlers and more units of veterans, some from World War II, some from Korea. The yellow sun strengthened, drawing water up off the pavement in waves of steam. A few puffy clouds hung high in a sky washed to a clean and sparkling blue. The neat rows of brick buildings that made up Liberty Hollow's tiny downtown might never have been touched by wind or rain.

Drenched parade watchers didn't steam-dry quite as quickly. Marnie pulled self-consciously at her T-shirt. Dampness kept it hugging her slight curves, and her hair had gotten plastered to her head and over her shoulders. It had lost the volume she'd added to the long strands this morning with styling goop and a curling iron. Instead of flowing smoothly back from her forehead, the honey-colored mass now fell into two sections that divided naturally at a center part.

The last band went by. It didn't play, but instead marked time with drums. *Boom, rat-a-tat, boom.* Marnie's imagination responded to the driving beat. The pounding sounded like thunder, then hail on a roof or the rattle of gunfire, then thunder again.

A street sweeper came next, its tanklike shape moving slowly from side to side of the asphalt to pick up the debris left by horses and spectators. Breezily Marnie said, "That seems to be all, guys, so—"

A group of former soldiers who had been hidden by the antics of the street sweeper sailed into view. While they were still a block away, Marnie paused in mid-sentence, her heart constricting. In contrast to the other marching units, the members of this one didn't seem to be making much effort to step in time. The fact that several were in wheelchairs might make the difference, she thought. Then she realized that the slovenly formation wasn't accidental but deliberate. It was a statement, just as the baggy jungle fatigues, worn instead of dress uniform, were a statement. And the communal glare the veterans turned on the citizens who lined the sidewalk spoke for itself.

"What's wrong with them?" asked Mark.

Marnie cleared her throat. "They fought in Vietnam."

"They did?" Kevin looked them over critically. "Kind of old."

"Not so old," Marnie contradicted him. "Late thirties to midforties, maybe."

"That's old," Kevin said positively.

Marnie smiled. "To you, I suppose it is. My big brother went to Vietnam." Unexpected tears stung behind her eyelids. It had been years since she'd cried for Bill. She blinked fiercely. "He didn't come back. But I guess I feel like any of those men could be my brother, so—so none of them seems that old to me."

"They're pretty lousy at marching," Mark remarked coolly.

"You try it from a wheelchair," Marnie snapped. She drew a breath. *Be fair*, she told herself. The boys hadn't been born—hadn't even been conceived—in '75. That was when the last American forces withdrew from Saigon. They had no shadowy memories of a tall, kind-voiced young man in an army uniform to remind them of a conflict most people wanted to forget. Carefully she added, "Their war wasn't popular. When the soldiers came home a lot of them were called horrible names and couldn't get jobs. Some of them are still mad about the way they were treated."

"So that's why those guys are at the end of the parade? Because they were in Vietnam?" asked Chad. The squad was approaching slowly behind a drooping flag.

The lady in the lawn chair cackled. "That's right. Parade committee had to let 'em march; din't haveta let 'em aggravate everybody else."

Marnie glanced around, feeling unusually helpless. The pall of sullen suspicion that hung over the squad was blasphemy in the sunshine, the laughter, the normalcy of Main Street in a town she'd known almost half her life. Depression and paranoia weren't her style, but, oh, God, how unfair this was. So many years of bitterness.... One of the men was navigating the tangle of camouflage fatigues like a tiger stalking through the jungle. His face was harsh but didn't appear bitter; it held the set expression of a man with a job to do, a job he hated but intended to get done.

Nobody should have to look like that when the job was just marching in a parade.

Something passionate and hot burned away the lingering smart of tears in Marnie's eyes. Jumping up, she signaled to Kevin and the others with an impatient hand. They stared at her.

"Get up! *Up.* Get that baseball cap off your head, Chad! Now!"

"Aw, Ms. Rainbrook—"

"Face forward. Do it!"

"Ms. Rainbrook, we'd look dumb. Nobody else—"

Furiously Marnie said, "Are you going to live all your lives doing only what other people do?"

They shuffled their feet in their brand name running shoes. Even Kevin. The whole lot of them stared down at the gutter. All five sat with the stubborn immobility only teenagers can attain.

Her throat tightened. The Oaks was an extremely expensive school. The parents of these kids certainly weren't paying the obscene tuition charged there to have a teacher lose her cool as if she were as fallible as the parents themselves. Marnie knew from experience—as a child, as a teacher—that troubled teenagers couldn't be guided by snarled orders. But . . . it could have been Bill out there in the street, made thin and angry by a year in hell and twenty years of hell's aftermath. And one lesson Marnie had learned in her own life was that the only cure for angry helplessness was to do something about it.

Tossing her hair out of her eyes, Marnie ignored the boys squatting in an uncomfortable circle around her and stood at proud attention. For a moment her hand wavered in the air; she wasn't quite sure where it should go. Of its own accord, it crept across her chest and placed itself over her heart.

JARED CAIN caught a glimpse of swirling taffy blond hair ahead and to his right, and forced himself to keep his gaze on the line running down the middle of the street. No point in looking, even though his neck and jaw muscles ached with tension and he would have welcomed the excuse to relax and change position. He knew what he would see. Smiling faces gradually losing all expression. Accusing stares. He heard nothing, at least nothing from the parade watchers. The only sound to penetrate the awkward stillness was a drumbeat from the band far in front of the squad, because the parade goers were falling into silence as his group came into sight.

Hell of a way to spend the first Saturday he'd had away from his desk in months. Independent brokerage houses didn't run themselves.

Ted Marshall jostled him. "Hey, Jerry, aren't you glad you came?"

He answered in the same undertone, learned a lifetime ago in boot camp. "Yeah. Thanks a million for the invitation. This town's so friendly. And who wouldn't want to relive the fab Nam era? Ideals disappearing in a puff of marijuana smoke, fun times crawling around in the jungle, the ecstasy of short arm drill—"

"Miniskirts," Ted offered. "Admit it, they made up for a lot."

It was impossible to stay grim around Ted. They'd met in a VA hospital, where Ted was being fitted with a new hand. "Yeah." Jared gave his friend half a smile. "You've got a point there."

Jared would never have met Ted if an unlucky private hadn't made a slight miscalculation. Sergeant Cain and the soldier had been working to defuse an explosive device . . .

At the memory, the narrow ridge of scar tissue that ran from his lower left eyelid to his jawline tried to twitch. It couldn't; there were too many nerve endings missing. But the sensation persisted. It was a frustrating tickle that wasn't quite an itch. He gave in to the compulsion to rub his cheek and make the nonfeeling go away.

With the movement, his head turned and he whistled softly. "Speaking of miniskirts—" But Ted had already wandered off to talk to one of the other guys, which was fine because amazement caused Jared to stop dead in his tracks.

A quick survey, from small feet in sandals to slender, well-shaped legs and then upward, revealed an attractive female body. The body was standing— standing with hand over heart in an old-fashioned gesture of respect. For the flag? For this ragtag troop of Nam vets? For *him?* His gaze didn't make it to her face; he watched in astonishment as a wave rippled outward from the woman, through the quiet spectators all the way down Main Street. In ones and twos, then in family groups, the parade watchers started hoisting themselves to their feet. Even the group of freshly scrubbed, sulky young thugs at the woman's feet scrambled up.

Slowly a trickle of applause swelled. Finally, all along the parade route as far as he could see, people were pounding their palms together as they stared at . . . his squad.

2

HE WAS DIMLY AWARE that the others in his group had halted, as he had. Most of them had their mouths open in astonishment.

Snapping his own teeth closed, Jared met the gaze of the woman who had started it all. *Young*, he thought. *Heartbreakingly young*. She had wide gray eyes shining with emotions he'd outgrown a long time ago. Optimism. Pure, shining hope. Joy.

For a split second, he thought he knew her from somewhere. The feeling gripped him so strongly that he raised his hand. His lips parted to call a greeting. Then reality hit. He'd never seen that gamine face or the subtly curved body that went with it before today; he would have remembered them with absolute clarity. Jared was sure of it. A man didn't forget that sort of sexuality, not overt but still unmistakable and compelling. However, the style of the woman—that was familiar.

It wasn't just the skirt. The denim was cut to mid-thigh and there was a fringe around the hem that pretended to cover the lightly tanned legs it drew attention to instead. It wasn't the T-shirt with some sort of symbol blazoned over small, high breasts. Or even her glorious hair, although not too many women wore their hair like that anymore. Center-parted, it hung without bangs nearly to her waist. All the girls had worn their hair like that the year he went to war. But that wasn't what teased his memory either.

No, the odd jolt of déjà vu had come from her expression—glowing and dedicated. She fairly burst with the kind of happy trust in the goodness of things that used to inspire folk songs and movements to save the world . . . before the faith—his faith, at least—had exploded in the blast from one private's mistake. The private hadn't even been scratched. Jared's own life had become a dreary round of hospitals.

After years of enduring doctors and operating rooms, he'd talked his way into college. For a lot of kids, it was an easy, irresponsible time. Already in his mid-twenties, he had found it a nearly unbearable grind. He'd had to teach himself how to limber a mind that had never bothered to study before. At the same time, Jared had learned to handle the inevitable awkwardness when he met people whose eyes skittered away at the sight of scars not yet reduced by reconstructive surgery. He'd learned how rarely others practiced the proverbs they preached. Most people really did judge a book by its cover. A man by his scars.

By his thirties his face had been put back together in a reasonable approximation of its original looks, and all his energy had gone into the tooth and nail scramble for success.

The big gray eyes continued to hold his. For the first time in a long time, Jared wished he still believed in pleasant, foolish things. Like essential decency. Or love.

Love? Oh, man, he wanted a cigarette.

His fingers twitched, and a feeling like an army of ants marching under his skin made him blink. He wanted a cigarette *bad*.

Damn, maybe the time had come to quit. Jared despised needing anything. It was a chink in his nearly perfect armor of self-sufficiency. He couldn't remember a nicotine fit this overpowering since his last operation, ten years ago.

Restlessly he took a step backward. It hit him that the parade was disappearing around a corner two blocks away, and he and the other guys still weren't moving.

"Hey, Barker!" he called quietly.

Barker, the flag bearer, stared at him bemusedly. The flagpole was slipping from his lax grasp. Stars and Stripes lay half submerged in the puddle of dirty water left by the street sweeper's brush. Jared didn't turn around, but he could feel the weight of those expectant gray eyes on his back. With an oath, he strode forward, wrenched the pole from Barker's unresisting grip and held it high.

"All right, soldiers, let's go." He gave a short laugh. "Parade march, you guys."

Holding her breath, Marnie watched the squad shape up. Wheelchairs came first, and then those who could walk formed up behind in two neat columns. The man who moved with a tiger's grace took his place at the front and led them forward in double-quick time. The flag billowed over his head.

Her lungs squeezed, pushing out air in a hard sigh. They were a magnificent bunch of men—rumpled uniforms, disabilities, bad attitudes and all. She felt light and happy all of a sudden. Her students had come through in a pinch. So had the town. And the leader of the soldiers . . . he'd been nothing short of wonderful.

"There's no more, Ms. Rainbrook," Mark said, bored. "This is the most hick town in the world. Can we go now?"

Marnie took his cap and set it backward on his head. "Nope. We have to wait for Mr. Simpson—oh, here he is. David, could you take the guys and help them enlarge their experience by exploring greater downtown Liberty Hollow for a while? I have something I want to do. I can meet you over at Bomben's soda fountain in an hour or so. I'll treat."

Although the students rolled their eyes in disgust, they went, shepherded by lanky, calm David Simpson. Marnie smiled to see Kevin react in the same way as the others; at least he had some normal teenage instincts. An aversion to rural townships seemed to be one of them. But the boys had healthy appetites—and rules at The Oaks kept pupils chronically short of spending money. She didn't doubt that when the time came, they'd be lined up at the soda fountain counter, enthusiastically arguing over the menu.

Not hesitating, she walked steadily in the opposite direction. The parade had gone this way.

It was over. Trudging toward her were tired-looking kids hugging band instruments. There were also clusters of beauty queens holding the trains of their long dresses with one hand and their tiaras with the other. Feeling like a salmon swimming upstream, Marnie pushed her hair out of her face with impatient fingers. The flossy stuff drifted down again. Generally she liked it long; somehow the thick, fine-textured mane fed her sense of being an individual. But every now and then Alice in Wonderland hair was a royal pain.

Sighing, she collapsed on the steps of the Carnegie Library and plumped her purse on her lap. Perhaps a barrette or an elasticized band lurked at the bottom.

Jared's good intentions to give up smoking lasted until he caught sight of the miniskirted young woman rooting in her bag. He'd kept an eye cocked for her in the chaos after the parade. It cheered him to discover that she smoked, too. Somehow a bad habit shared was a bad habit absolved. He clapped a hand on Ted's back and said, "See you in a few minutes, okay?" Not waiting for a reply, he maneuvered his way through the throng of townspeople milling in front of the library. He pulled out a battered pack of cigarettes.

"Looking for one of these?"

She looked up, and Jared thought, *She's lovely.*

Not classically beautiful, though. Her bone structure was too strong for mere prettiness, and as he'd noted before, the lines of her figure were coltish, not voluptuous. Her face was free of makeup. But then, this woman didn't need any. Her eyes were extraordinary without it—a clear, true gray with long lashes that darkened at the tips. In contrast to her stubborn cheekbones and chin, her naked mouth was soft, very soft. Kissable.

Her gaze fell from his face to the pack. "Um, no. No, thank you."

"Don't like the brand?" Jared shook one out and lit it, almost in one motion. He sat companionably next to her. His longer legs stretched a step past hers. He didn't try to control a male impulse to study the way the fringe of her skirt sifted over her neat thighs.

She seemed fascinated with the first small cloud of white smoke that escaped his lips and dissipated into the sparkling air. "I don't know anything about brands. I've never smoked."

Jared transferred the cigarette to the hand away from her. "Sorry. I saw you stirring around in your purse and made an assumption. Stupid of me."

She smiled in a friendly way. "No, it was kind of you to offer. Actually, I like the smell, and I'm not too worried about the occasional dose of passive smoke. It's probably just as dangerous to hang around a barbecue. Sniffing lighter fluid and carcinogens rising off the meat can't be terribly good for you. But I do it every summer. I mean, honestly, I don't mind cigarettes."

His answering grin was a brief thinning of the lips. "Life's too short to worry about prolonging it."

"Not a very cheerful thought."

He shrugged broad shoulders. "Nobody's perfect. I'm Jared Cain."

"Marnie Rainbrook. Hi." Silence stretched between them, a not entirely comfortable silence.

No woman with any intuitive femininity could have missed Jared's lazy perusal of her legs. It pleased Marnie with an intensity that startled her; she'd been wishing for an attractive man to give her just that kind of ego-affirming, discreetly lascivious glance, but . . . this particular attractive man wasn't some pale fantasy. He was tall and dark and lean, as well as cynical from the sound of it. The seam of an old scar added danger to his face.

To break the silence, she said, "To tell you the truth, I did try smoking once. I was around twelve. I hid in the bathroom, which was a good thing because as soon as I took a puff, I threw up. And up. Even the hope of annoying my father and stepmother—by developing an addiction they'd hate—couldn't get me to try again . . ."

Her voice trailed off as she realized the story wasn't the most tactful one she could have chosen to entertain a man who smoked. But Jared surprised her by laughing out loud. It was a deep, rich sound. A crooked smile changed his finely drawn features, taking years off his face.

Another inordinate rush of pleasure flashed through her. He lifted brows that she'd already realized were usually knit into a frown over eyes the same color as his hair—brown with coppery highlights. But where his hair, cut in a professional style, looked touchable, the eyes inspecting her held a hard glint.

His quiet, rather husky voice was kindly, though. "You're lucky, Marnie Rainbrook. Upchucking the first time you light one of these is a good survival response."

"You know about things like that? Survival?" Marnie asked with interest. She'd taken wilderness survival courses in college.

She couldn't stop staring at him. Grooves cut deep into his cheeks whenever he smiled or frowned. His scar ran neatly parallel to one of them. At the outer edges of his dark eyes the skin puckered from the weight of his continually lowered brows.

Jared brushed a piece of ash from his camouflage pants. "If I didn't, I wouldn't be here now."

His careful lack of inflection underlined the significance of his scar and battle uniform. Her experience of surviving couldn't be the same as his at all, she thought. Hot color flooded Marnie's face. Though her family had accused her of being too direct on enough occasions for her to know the indictment must be true, she wasn't about to burst out and say, *I'm sorry you were injured,* or *I'm glad you didn't get killed all those years ago because otherwise I wouldn't have gotten to meet you.*

Embarrassed, she produced at random, "I was looking for you." The words sparked in the air between them. Abruptly she realized how what she'd actually said must sound. Her flush burned hotter than ever.

For some Freudian reason, the revealing sentence had rolled out of her mouth. A graduate of The Oaks never evaded consequences—no matter how much she might like to, just this once, Marnie thought—so she hooked a wandering strand of blond hair behind her ear and faced him. Not for her, hiding behind the convenience of a ready-made curtain of hair.

Marnie—*Marnie*, he liked that—had the most delicious blush, Jared was thinking. Instead of round splotches high on her cheekbones or overall redness, her blush took the form of banners of dusky rose. The banners were longer than they were wide, like splashes of watercolor under her fresh complexion.

"Looking for me?" he repeated, lighting another cigarette from the butt of the first. She blushed like a virgin. She looked like lost innocence. Jared dragged smoke into his lungs to fill them with something familiar.

At the last moment, he remembered to blow the cloud away from Marnie. She smiled faintly. Jared wondered if she could tell he was having a devil of a time keeping his eyes off her.

"Yes," she said more easily. "I wanted to let you know how much I admired what you did today. Taking part in the parade, picking up the flag, everything."

"No big deal," he replied, shrugging.

"It was to me." When she swallowed, the muscles in her smooth throat constricted and then relaxed. Jared found himself watching, trying to decide where her skin would be most sensitive. When he held the cigarette away, the fresh scent of her perfume seduced him into wondering how she'd taste. Clean and, oh, so sexy.

"You're an idealist."

"Please, that's practically an insult in this day and age," Marnie protested. "But I believe there are things that are important. And the people who do them are special. You did something special today."

There must be something wrong with him. The day, maybe, and all the sentiment. Detours down memory lane were generally mistakes, he thought with a resurgence of the cynicism that was like an old friend. It had been a long time since he'd hung around with other vets in any numbers. Or sat in the sun next to a girl with hair like a waterfall of silk brushing against his arm.

Blushing blondes weren't his type. He usually chose experienced, together women close to his own age who expected no more from him than he did from them . . . women who'd been around enough not to expect physical perfection—any kind of perfection—in a lover; sexual partners as cynical as he was. Casual relationships were easily made and painlessly broken.

Vaguely recalled from college, Ben Franklin's suggestion on how to choose a mistress ran through his mind: It's better to make an older woman grateful than a young woman miserable. *Randy old reprobate*, Jared reflected. Sound advice.

Coolly he said, "It seemed like a good idea to get moving. Nam vets are usually at the end of whatever line is forming. No sense in getting left behind altogether. A little too symbolic of the way we tend to be treated."

"I know." The gray eyes sought his. "My brother was killed in the last year of the war. While the parade was going on, I thought about what it would have been like for him if he'd lived. He was such a kind, easygoing guy when he left. It's horrible to imagine him coming home to so much hostility. I wish he could be here, though."

"You had a brother in Nam? How old?" Jared demanded.

"Bill was eleven years older than me. He enlisted right out of high school."

Some quick mental arithmetic pulled Jared's mouth to one side. He watched her looking at his scar. His smile only had one side. "You must be about twenty-four."

"Uh-huh." The shining eyes smiled, as if the scar were nothing. Or a—a freckle. Or anything that was an ordinary part of a human face. He was very aware of the road map of ruined skin engraved on his chest, currently covered by his old camouflage shirt. Surgery hadn't been able to do much to reduce those scars. She said equably, "And you're—"

"Forty."

Damn, didn't anything faze her? Marnie Rainbrook acted as if the difference in their ages didn't exist. She parked her elbows on her shapely knees and continued to drill him with a total lack of inhibition that sank his resolve to get up and stroll away. She was too young, too reckless with her trust. She got too easily under his skin. The slow simmer of sensual awareness continued to tease him. Her breasts poked out the front of her T-shirt like little teepees, small and firm and pointed. Cute.

In response to her questions, he told her he'd been a sergeant of emergency ordinance disposal. "We blew up bombs that happened to be in the wrong places, sprang little surprises the enemy left for our guys in the jungle, stuff like that," he explained.

"Wow. That's quite a specialty. Do you ever get calls for help from police or bomb squads or anybody like that?"

"I don't advertise what I did for the army," he answered with sudden curtness. "I'm not in the business of hiring myself out to handle other people's dirty odd jobs like a soldier of fortune."

She absorbed his snappish tone without flinching. Damn, she was sweet. "So, what do you do for a living?"

"Shoot craps with God." That got to her; she did a double take. He laughed at her expression. "I own half a commodities brokerage in Chicago. We deal in things like farm futures. Guessing what the weather will be like in Iowa in July, so we can decide what to pay for crops that haven't been harvested yet."

"I know what futures are," Marnie told him. Jared must be a high roller. If the stock market as a whole was the respectable equivalent of gambling, commodities were the highest risk game. A hundred dinner table lectures from her childhood surfaced and she said, "You like living dangerously."

"Not at all," he denied. "I'm about as middle class as you can get. I live by the rules. The rules pay pretty good. Most days I strangle myself in a tie and spend ten hours on the phone or hunched over a computer."

Leaning back against the next step, Marnie flicked her eyes over him critically. Wiry muscles over big bones. If an ounce of excess fat covered that sprawling body, she'd resign as a physical education instructor. "You're a liar, Sergeant Cain," she said with the forthrightness so deplored by her family. "What is it with you, racquetball?"

A tinge of respect crept into his husky voice. "That's clever of you. Yeah, I work in three, four games a week. At night, mostly. How'd you guess?"

"Your color's good, very good for a smoker, but not deeply tanned. I can't believe you're the kind of man to slather himself in sunscreen, so tennis is out. Same applies to golf. Besides, I'd say golf is too slow for someone like you."

He lifted quizzical brows. "Like me?"

"Well, let's say if you roll dice with God you must enjoy battling odds. So you probably go for fast games with visible results. In racquetball there's always a winner and a loser—I'll bet you're usually the winner—it's played indoors and it's great for staying in shape."

Jared pitched the stub of his cigarette into a stone urn and turned toward her, leaning on his elbow. His shadow covered her. With a small shock, Marnie realized she didn't feel any impulse to back away. All those hours of self-defense lessons, all the cautionary tales a smart woman took seriously about never letting a stranger get too close . . . none of them applied to this stranger.

Ridiculous even to imagine cause for alarm here in the sunlight. They were within calling distance of a lot of nice people who'd come running at a squeak, let alone a yell. And at a level so basic she couldn't doubt it, Marnie knew Jared wasn't going to hurt her. At least not on purpose. If danger lurked, it was in the indefinable pull she felt coming from him. Marnie wasn't stupid. Her modus operandi never varied. Cautious friendliness around new animals and new people. Yet here she was, almost surrounded by a man in jungle garb, with wary jungle eyes that glinted as if they wanted—he wanted—to eat her right up. . . .

Jared had to admit to himself it was a distinct pleasure to hear a lovely blonde tell him she thought he was in great shape. "You know a lot about sports," he congratulated her. Another perusal confirmed slender wrists and no bulky muscles. "On the other hand, you don't look much like a jock."

Her laughter matched the rest of her appearance, soft and silvery. "Don't say that; you'll get me fired. I teach physical education and do some—well, sort of counseling at a school near here."

"You teach phys ed? To those hulks I saw you with down the street?"

"They're some of my students, yes. We're coed. I just happen to be one of the boys', uh, homeroom teachers."

It was never easy to translate the unique conditions at The Oaks into traditional terms, so Marnie didn't try. Time enough to reveal that she didn't teach any regularly scheduled classes. Instead, her job was to devise situations that would impart physical and emotional survival skills to intelligent, troubled teens who would be in juvenile hall if they hadn't been lucky enough to land somewhere like The Oaks.

"So what kind of phys ed do you specialize in? Don't tell me. You're the football coach, right?" Disbelief still threaded through his voice, although his mouth had relaxed into a more authentic-looking smile.

"You're really sexist, aren't you?" Marnie asked tolerantly.

Jared seemed to consider the charge, crossing his ankles. "Not about most things. I'm willing to let a woman open her own doors. If one steals a taxi from me I swear at her the same as I would at a man."

"Gee, you're a great guy, Sarge."

He ignored her laughing comment. "I advance women on my professional staff, and if I wanted to work for someone else—which I don't—a female boss would be fine. But I can't say I'm wild about the thought of—" He caught himself just in time, before he said *you*. It would be ridiculous to get personal after less than an hour's acquaintance. "I'm not wild about any woman being tackled by some kid who's seventy pounds heavier than she is."

Marnie decided not to tell him that the proper word wasn't *tackled* but *attacked*. For some reason, the information that she held a black belt in karate had a tendency to send potential dates into hasty retreat. Not that Jared Cain gave the impression he backed away from a fight. Quite the contrary. Even lounging on library steps, surely the most civilized thing to do in the world, he looked capable of springing into instant, deadly action.

But Marnie didn't want to fight with him. In fact, the prospect of seeing more of Jared was causing odd little tingles to skip along her nerve endings.

"I can handle myself," she said, crossing an arm over her chest and rubbing her shoulder in reaction to the tingling feeling. His gaze followed the motion. To her surprise, the fact that he was watching her made her experience her own touch as reflective and . . . sensual. She stopped her hand and quickly added, "I can handle the kids, too. They're my job, and I love my students. I'm not much for team sports, though. Not good at them."

"None?" He studied her inscrutably.

"Nope." It took a moment for Marnie to realize he might be talking about sex. Though she felt a fresh wave of heat flood her cheeks she didn't change her answer. Sex wasn't a game to her.

His eyes narrowed to slits. "You're a real puzzle, Marnie Rainbrook," he murmured. "What are you doing blushing your way through a world where everybody looks out for number one?"

It wasn't the kind of comment that was easy to answer. "I'm stuck with thin skin," she said finally. "It's my burden in life."

He flicked a finger over her cheek, and it seemed natural to Marnie to let him. "Your skin's like velvet," he said under his breath. Marnie didn't breathe at all.

Jared sighed and turned half away from her, lighting another cigarette. "A teacher. It fits."

Marnie's lungs began to pump air in and out again. She concentrated on taking slow, even breaths to counteract the feeling she'd been starved of oxygen for a week. "What's that mean?"

"Wide-eyed idealistic types go into teaching," he said with the hint of a patronizing drawl. "Or social work."

She forced herself to speak with precision. "First of all, I wish you'd stop calling me an idealist as if I had rose-colored glasses welded to my nose. Believing people can learn isn't normally considered a character flaw. Second, all the teachers and social workers I know are hard-working realists. They have to be, or the system uses them up and spits them out. Third, I'm not a *type*. I'm a person."

His brown eyes laughed at her. If copper was pounded impossibly thin and a light placed behind it, she thought, it would be exactly that color. "I can tell you're a person, Marnie Rainbrook. Is it okay if I say being a teacher suits you?"

It was an apology of sorts, Marnie supposed. Being accused of idealism wasn't so bad. It was Jared's tone that made it clear he didn't intend the label as a compliment. But holding grudges wasn't her style.

"Yes, it's okay," she said obligingly. One of the townspeople ran up the steps next to her so closely she could hear coins jingle in his pocket. "We seem to be hogging a thoroughfare. Would you like to join me for a cup of coffee? Or a drink or something? Beer?"

This time the thick brows didn't rise, they lowered even farther. "You're going to tell me you swig beer in the middle of the day?"

"Not usually," she admitted. "I was being adaptable. I didn't know what you'd prefer."

Jared knew what his preference would be. A vision of Marnie, with her hair spilled around her on the steps and her arms raised to pull him down into a cool embrace, was fleeting but so precisely detailed he sat up to hide his body's swift reaction. It had been years since spontaneous desire had threatened to embarrass him in public. Normally he could summon the sensations of arousal at will or ignore them when they weren't appropriate.

Live and learn.

He studied the grooves cut into the base of the stone urn with an intent interest they had probably failed to inspire in anyone except their sculptor. When the sense of fullness faded, he allowed himself to look at Marnie again.

His arousal, and his determined suppression of it, had taken only half a minute; she was still smiling at him with head tilted enquiringly. Her hand was raised to keep a sheaf of hair from falling across her face. Golden highlights and bronze shadows shifted as her fingers combed into the silky stuff to secure it in place. There was sexual awareness in her gaze; her eyes flickered from his eyes to his mouth and back again. What he didn't detect was desperation. Nor did she show bravado, or any of the emotions that typically afflicted the couple of women who had asked him out before.

Her composure reminded him again of the sixteen years that rose like a wall between them. Half a generation. A world of experiences they didn't share. Women his age hadn't mastered the mechanics of asking for a date without feeling brave or foolish. Obviously Marnie had grown up listening to fairy tales in which the princess went hunting for the prince. She looked cool as a cucumber...a very slender, sexy cucumber.

"I'll bet you don't even remember the Beatles," he said dryly.

Surprise softened her mouth for a moment. Jared repressed a desire to lean forward and discover how soft the pink curves really were. Then she grinned, showing small, pearly teeth. "Of course I remember them. How can you have a proper appreciation for current music without a thorough grounding in primitive rock and roll?"

"Primitive—"

Her laugh rang out. "I couldn't resist! I'm twenty-four, not fourteen. Of age, Sarge. I've heard of the Beatles. I can assure you I've got a valid Indiana state driver's license, so if you're worried about me not being able to produce ID in a bar, don't be."

"Get carded a lot, do you?" he asked with a reluctant grin.

"Whenever I order a drink," she admitted cheerfully. "I used to hate having to show proof of my age, but lately I've wondered if it won't be worse when bartenders can tell I'm over the hill in a low light."

Jared couldn't help it. He took her stubborn chin in his palm and turned the striking face to his. "Hardly over the hill."

A man could fall into those eyes and never find his way out. Never *want* to find his way out.

"Actually, I have to drive with my students back to school in a while. It would have to be coffee or a soda for me. But you can have a beer or whatever. So, Sarge," she said softly, "can I buy you a drink or not?"

A heavy arm suddenly draped itself over Jared's shoulder with enough force to surprise a grunt from him.

"Jerry!" Ted Marshall's hearty voice boomed. "I didn't realize you knew anybody in this burg. Especially not somebody gorgeous." Ted lowered his tone, not low enough. "Hey, man, who's the young babe?"

3

JARED PERFORMED brusque introductions.

"I always did have a lousy sense of timing," said Ted, removing his arm. His knowing grin remained tacked firmly in place, however.

"You're right," Jared agreed evenly.

Flashing him a glance, Marnie quickly asked, "Wonderful parade, wasn't it?"

She and Ted made small talk about the weather and the town while Jared thought, *Hell*. He'd been about to accept Marnie's invitation. He felt slightly guilty about it, but how often did lovely, funny, leggy blondes with trusting eyes and ideals worn on their sleeves sit down in a man's path? If the man was Jared, he admitted to himself, today was the first time. And he wasn't snatching her from the cradle, either, he told his conscience. Self-possessed Marnie had asked him out, not the other way around.

While he tried to quiet the small internal policeman that insisted this young woman ought to be going out with a young man and not a battle-scarred and world-weary cynic like him, Ted was making bad worse. "Jerry always did know how to optimize a situation. That's army talk. I don't suppose you've got a sister at home? With the same taste in clothes, slightly different taste in men?" Ted was the same height as Jared, but carried fifty pounds more on his heavy frame. His old uniform literally bulged at the seams.

"'Fraid not." Despite Ted's friendly leer, Marnie wasn't blushing now, Jared noted.

Then she met Jared's gaze. Pretty color streaked her cheeks.

She feels it, too, Jared thought. An awareness of mutual attraction too new to be comfortable. A liking for what each had discovered of the other so far. A definite hint of lust.

No way was he going to expose so many untried emotions to Ted's genial interference.

"Marnie," he said, "I promised Ted and the guys to spend the afternoon swapping war stories. Maybe we could share a drink another time. I hope you understand."

"Yes, of course." Damn it all, he'd done it—put a brave smile on her lips. He bent his neck, trying to catch her gaze again, but she began to fuss with her purse and kept her head down.

"Well, I don't understand," said Ted roundly. "Marnie can come with us. The other guys'll know how to appreciate her even if you don't. Cripes, Jer, I was bragging on you. You'll make me look nohow if you can't pick up a girl better than that."

The grim lines of Jared's face grew perceptibly grimmer. As she had when Ted had plopped himself down next to them on the steps and she'd sensed Jared's annoyance at the interruption, Marnie hurried into speech. "That's okay. I have a bunch of kids to round up, anyway. This is really a work day for me."

"That's terrible." Earnestness sat well on Ted's full face. "It's a Saturday. In June. Nobody should work today."

She shook her head. "Teachers in residential schools work around the clock. So if you'll excuse me...."

She glanced sideways at Jared. Something had started between them, she was sure of it. Perhaps he didn't want it to go any further. Perhaps—oh, God, he could be married. His strong-looking fingers were free of rings, but a lot of men didn't wear wedding rings.

The embarrassing possibility existed that he'd been shocked when she'd asked him to join her for a drink. Invitations, female-to-male rather than male-to-female, certainly weren't unheard of, though Marnie had never felt the need to resort to one before. Promptly she decided she'd never do so again. It was distinctly un-fun to get turned down. Men had been suffering all these centuries. She'd never sympathized properly.

Besides, it didn't seem likely that she'd run into another man who would attract her with that same unexpected swiftness. After all, it had never happened before. There was no particular reason to assume it would again.

Still, it had been nice for a brief half-hour to bask in a man's hot, unapologetic admiration. A dream fulfilled. But the fantasy was over now.

Jared watched her. It seemed to him that she quietly withdrew, switching off her subtle sexuality. Her body language altered in small ways. Lashes swept down to cover suddenly clouded gray eyes. Her straight spine curved even as her shoulders straightened. Tapering fingers with short, clean nails closed over her purse.

She stood up. Instead of continuing to sit so he could enjoy the sight of her legs—a decided temptation—he uncoiled to his feet.

Another spasm of guilt twisted somewhere in the vicinity of his heart. The sensation must be guilt, he thought in surprise; it had been so long since his heart had been pummeled by love, he assumed it was dead to the feeling.

"It was nice meeting you both—" Her smile was bright and undiminished.

"Wait," Jared said. "Can I have your phone number?"

She looked up at him, perplexed, searching his face for clues to why he was asking. He stood perhaps seven inches taller than she, and what she saw was six-feet-and-a-bit of frowning and formidable man. What had happened to turn the lounging cat into the angry lion?

Besides, if he didn't want to see more of her this afternoon, why should he want to call her later?

Ted coughed, and began to sound more like a smooth-talking professional, which he was. For ten years, he'd been the other half of Cain and Marshall. "You know, if you two want to be alone to discuss the ramifications of commitment involved in giving out a phone number . . ."

The amusement in his remark made Marnie realize how long she'd been staring into Jared's taut face. She started. "No! I mean, I can be reached at The Oaks." Self-consciously, she pointed to the fancy script that decorated the spreading tree pictured on her T-shirt. "Directory assistance can give you the number. The switchboard will put you through or take a message if I'm away from the buildings."

Jared raked his gaze over the T-shirt as if memorizing a masterpiece. Marnie just plain couldn't figure him out. If he liked what he saw, why turn down her perfectly straightforward invitation for a drink?

And men said women were incomprehensible.

The part of Ted's belly unrestrained by the waistband under his open shirt shook. His voice, however, had become politely bland. "You don't have a phone at home?"

"The Oaks *is* my home," she explained, dragging her attention from Jared. She repeated her edited information to Ted.

"You mean like a boarding school?" he asked incredulously.

"Bite your tongue. That's an outdated phrase. The buzzword today is *residential* school." To herself she added, "Evil stepmothers, take note."

"What?"

"Nothing." She smiled at both men. "Well, be seeing you."

Jared stepped smoothly into her path, his lean body somehow neatly angled to block the sidewalk. His unexpected movement brought Marnie to a halt almost in his arms. She meant to step back, but from a pocket he conjured a cream-colored card.

"In case you want to reach me," he said.

For an annoyed moment, Marnie wondered if he was rubbing in the fact that she'd more or less made a pass at him . . . and been turned down. But his brown gaze held hers steadily, and he didn't look like a man trying to hide a laugh. Slowly, Marnie lifted her hand to take the card. Her fingers brushed his knuckles. They felt smooth and hard, the skin over them warm. She pulled her hand back quickly.

"Goodbye again," murmured Marnie, and forced herself to step around him. Most of her hour was up, and Bomben's was at the other end of the street.

"Only you would keep business cards in your old jungle bunny uniform," Ted said.

Jared replied with a grunt. Marnie's neat bottom undulated in the slim skirt as she walked away. She had a decisive stride, he noted. Well, of course, she must have athletic ability if she taught phys ed. But she certainly didn't suffer from either the stockiness or the stringiness he associated with female athletes. Her walk had a springy quality to it. He wondered how strong those slender legs really were. Would lovemaking make them grip a man as if they'd never let him go?

Ted sighed. "Life's not such a bitchin' proposition after all. Miniskirts are back."

Ted's appreciation for the jaunty sway of Marnie's tasseled hem ruffled Jared. He opened his mouth to snap something crude about voyeurs, and then realized how ridiculous his surge of jealousy really was.

After all, he'd been looking, too. And he'd known Marnie for maybe an hour. A rather short time to be harboring territorial instincts.

Ted was his friend, had been for years. Okay, so his partner didn't deserve to be snapped at. Jared still didn't like the way the other man's gaze was following Marnie's pert little backside. Swallowing his original comment, he purposefully distracted Ted by asking, "What's The Oaks, anyway? *Are* there Victorian institutions like boarding schools around anymore?"

"Apparently. I could find out about this place for you. My brother-in-law works for a school district. I'll get him to make a call," Ted replied. He gave Marnie's swaying fringe a last, fond look as she entered a storefront. "If you like."

"Yeah," said Jared slowly. "I'd like."

"Consider it done. Aren't you glad you came to the parade? Never can figure what you're going to find growing out here in the corn and soybean belt."

ACRES OF CORN rustled in the breeze. The stiff leaves and thin stalks rubbed together, making a whispering sound.

A *ninja* warrior wearing a black tunic and pants liberally spotted with brown paint, and with a blue arm band knotted above his elbow, stepped into a break in the shifting stalks. Then he glided back behind the corn in the space of a heartbeat.

Marnie spotted the fleeting form and grinned. Her perch atop The Oaks' old tractor provided an excellent view of the adjoining field, where the corn grew tall enough to provide concealment for all the *ninjas* in today's war game.

"The problem was in the gas intake," Kevin said from beside her. The seat they shared had been built for one. Happily the designer had expected that one to be a farmer with substantial haunches. Both Marnie and Kevin were rather small through that area, so though room on the seat was cramped, it was sufficient. Marnie barely noticed. Kevin's eyes were bright, he'd said more today than he had in the entire three weeks she'd been working with him, and he'd stayed focused on a practical, doable project all morning.

"Uh-huh."

"That's why you were getting those jerky starts and stops. When I fixed that, I took a look at the ignition . . ."

With one ear devoted to the boy's enthusiastic catalog of repairs he'd made, Marnie let some of her attention drift back to the cornfield.

Her sixteenth summer had been devoted to working these same fields. She loved the smell of the rich loam. And the panorama of greens—green stalks, green leaves with lighter veining that made them look like watered silk—gave her a deep sense of satisfaction. Originally, she'd set up today's war game to run itself. She was supposed to be using the morning to plan an upcoming camping trip, but Marnie was glad she'd given in to Kevin's request to play hooky from her office. He'd wanted to show off what he'd done to the tractor. The only reason she'd grabbed an arm band was so he wouldn't feel alone in the midst of the game. She had the feeling Kevin felt like that all too often.

"You know, Ms. Rainbrook," said Kevin with a man-to-helpless-woman arrogance Marnie found rather touching in a fourteen-year-old, "I can keep this heap running. No problem. But why can't the school buy a new tractor? And I'd better warn you, you'll get in trouble if my dad finds out you're letting me get axle grease under my fingernails. He says that's for dumb-bells, only he calls me—I mean, them—underachiev-ers."

"You're awfully good at mechanical things." With such compliments, Marnie hoped to nourish the seed-lings of his self-esteem.

"Dad wants me to go into one of the sciences—phys-ics or something." Kevin said it with a dull hopeless-ness that told its own story.

Marnie made a mental note to put a line in his file encouraging the headmaster to speak to Kevin's father. In the meantime, she said, "Things'll turn out okay if you try hard enough. Wait and see."

Kevin adjusted his orange arm band, which matched the one Marnie wore over the sleeve of her blue cotton blouse. His expression of cynical amusement re-minded her of the man she'd met yesterday, Jared Cain. She shook her head with irritation. The ex-soldier had popped into her mind several times already. "If you say so, Ms. Rainbrook. Anyway, if my dad catches me fixing the school's tractor, he's going to want a discount on the tuition."

Marnie laughed. "Sounds like my dad." She didn't tell him the ancient piece of machinery was a valuable part of the curriculum, kept around for students like him—kids with good hands and good brains and a desperate lack of common sense. A Kevin who was tinkering with a tractor wasn't out stealing spare parts in order to build an automatic pistol.

"Old, small tractors are better for the soil, anyway," she went on. "Less compaction, so it's looser and less eroded."

"You care a lot about environmental stuff, don't you?" Kevin clutched at the medallion around his neck.

"Well, I think we've got a nice little planet here, with a lot of wear left in it if we treat it right," Marnie replied lightly. "What's that medal you're always wearing? It's awfully impressive."

"My dad gave it to me." He held the embossed circle of silver out at the end of its chain so Marnie could inspect it. "He won it at some big national science fair when he was my age." Kevin's tone revealed both pride and helplessness. Pride in his father's achievements, she thought. Helpless recognition that he'd never match them? Kevin was definitely a square peg having trouble fitting into somebody else's round hole. Marnie knew how that felt.

"Oh. It's—" she broke off. A patch of baggy black pants betrayed the whereabouts of the *ninja* in the corn.

Silently Marnie pointed. Kevin peered, then looked back at her in confusion. She could tell he'd missed the telltale blot of simple monochromatic color, so rare in nature. Signaling to him to reach for his paint gun, she bent and picked up hers from beneath her feet. When they both straightened, she put a light fingertip under his chin and directed his gaze to the *ninja*, who had to be an enemy from the blue team. It might be Chad, she guessed, from the wide build.

Kevin went tense under her matter-of-fact touch—so tense that she was afraid the boy's jaw had locked from simple stress. "Kevin?" she barely whispered. "Are you all right?"

He knocked her hand away from his chin. Marnie gasped, then bit her lip. Isolated Kevin probably wasn't used to a friendly touch. Possibly the poor little guy didn't know how to react to one. Forcing herself to relax and smile, she asked, "Ready to get him?" in an attempt to make up for her gaffe.

His black head nodded, but he wouldn't look at her.

They waited, a tense minute stretching out until Marnie could feel a drop of perspiration trickle slowly between her breasts. It tickled and felt cold. Restlessly she remembered Jared Cain's leisurely contemplation of that area of her anatomy. He *had* been attracted to her; all the signals had been there. It couldn't have been clearer if the man had hired a billboard and painted, "I lust after Marnie Rainbrook," in letters fifteen feet tall.

But in an equally obvious way, he'd signalled rejection.

"Hi-ya!" A *ninja* burst from the wall of corn into the open field. The plowed dirt made for a soggy, shifting surface, and he went sprawling facedown. Marnie jerked her paint rifle to her shoulder. Her quick shot sent a gush of washable paint sinking into the earth where the *ninja*—it was Chad—would have been had he not fallen.

A splatter hit her back with enough force to push her forward so her chest touched her knees.

Sitting up again, she looked over her shoulder and raised her brows at Kevin. "What was that for? I thought we were on the same team."

He smiled with deprecating charm. "Bang," he said, and pulled off his orange arm band to reveal the blue one that had been hidden underneath.

Marnie's grimace apparently struck the boys as exquisitely funny. Both of them lost the lower tones their voices had begun to develop, and whooped and giggled like seven-year-olds. "Great," said Marnie disgustedly, "just great."

Actually, Kevin and Chad's alliance made her happy. When Kevin had asked her to join him this morning, he must already have been part of a conspiracy. Good. Maybe he'd begun to make some friends. There was nothing like a shared enemy to create bosom buddies out of people who otherwise had little in common.

Did she have anything in common with Jared Cain, she found herself wondering. An hour hadn't been enough time to find out. Except for the fact he liked taking risks, and so did she. No, that wasn't quite right. Marnie loved the excitement of exploring challenges. But if Jared, a commodities broker, enjoyed outguessing the possible disasters that could influence the price of raw materials, then what he liked would be raw danger. The exhilaration of pitting himself against high odds.

Her grimace became genuine as she considered what her father's reaction would be to the news that his daughter had met and struck sparks with, of all things, a commodities broker. The only lower form of life in Arthur Rainbrook's world was the junk bond dealer.

In his long career as an investment banker, Marnie's father had never recommended purchasing anything but blue chip, absolutely safe sure things. He was a completely different corporate animal from Jared Cain.

Her scowl smoothed into a rueful smile. Arthur wasn't apt to find out. She was glad. It kept her from having to wonder if part of her attraction to long, lean, ex-army, all male Sergeant Cain could be the fact that he was definitely a man her family would never approve of.

"I really fooled you, huh, Ms. Rainbrook?" Kevin demanded.

"You sure did. I was completely sandbagged. Good work."

"You've got green hair!" he pointed out gleefully.

"Yippee," Marnie said drily. Pulling her braid forward, she inspected the paint that clotted its tip. It wasn't the soothing green of growing things, but a loud yellow-green that screamed its presence. Of course, that was the paint's purpose. Once splattered, a player in the war game was officially out. "I think I'll go back to my office and plot my revenge."

And find out if maybe, just maybe, Jared Cain had called. . . .

4

"HASN'T THE PUNK LOOK gone out of style?" asked David, glancing up from his desk. He and Marnie shared a cubbyhole of an office in the administration building.

Marnie dropped into one of the overstuffed chairs she'd brought in to make the office homey. The attempt at interior decoration worked; the office *was* homier. But with two bookcases, two desks, two rollaway chairs and two wing-backed chairs, it was also crowded. She propped her feet on her chair's twin. The hot weather had dried the paint on her back, so she didn't worry about the gaily patterned upholstery.

"What—don't you like my hair?" She waggled the end of her braid at him. "And I thought green was my color."

"Believe me, that shade of green isn't anybody's color," he answered, getting up to fill a glass of water for her from the cooler.

"Hey, where's that paint-ball catalog?" Her side of the desk was cluttered, as usual, but she could see at a glance that the colorful brochure wasn't where she'd left it. "It had some great diagrams in it. You know, explaining how the technology works."

"One of the kids wanted to look at it. Kevin, or Mark, or somebody." David handed her the glass. "You and those paint-ball games. I know you think they channel aggression—"

It was an argument they had frequently, comfortable as an old shoe. "Today we're channeling hormones," she interrupted. "Too bad you had to visit the dentist and miss the parade yesterday. You should have seen the boys with their tongues hanging out at those majorettes. They were pumped the rest of the day."

"And far into the night. I broke up a fight between Mark and Chad at about two a.m." David supervised the boys' dorm.

Dunking her braid into the water, she said, "Oh, no. You think taking them into town was a stinky idea then?"

He gave her his slow smile. Sometimes Marnie wondered why she didn't fall in love with David. He was gentle and clever, and only a few years older than she was. Nothing about his looks repelled her. In fact, he was quite attractive in a stoop-shouldered, academic way.

"It was a fine idea. There were circumstances not under your control. Mark's been agitating to go home. When we got back, a letter from his parents was waiting for him saying no way. So he was looking for a target to take his frustration out on. And Chad's been spoiling for a fight with somebody since his mom remarried. Bad timing, is all."

"Well, we've got to deal with their excess energy." She pulled her hair out of the glass and inspected it. Most of the green had dissolved into the water. "How about moving up the date of the camp-out? If you nag them with me, we could have the whole group ready to roll tomorrow bright and early."

Knowing that David's thought processes were deliberate and it would take him a few minutes to make up his mind, Marnie stood up and stretched. The thick, vegetable-based paint on her back clung, then cracked. She added, "I think I'll go shower and change my blouse." Going to the door, she hesitated and then closed it instead of going out. "David, we're friends, right?"

He looked vaguely surprised. "Right."

"So tell me something. We've gone out a couple of times. Why haven't you ever kissed me?"

His brows raised until they almost disappeared into his receding hairline. "Did you want me to?"

"Well . . ." She frowned in thought. "No, I guess I didn't. And I don't know why. You're my type. I like you. A lot."

The corners of his mouth barely quivered, but she got the impression he was laughing at her. "It's mutual. But just liking isn't enough. I seriously doubt I'm your type at all."

"Of course you are. You're nice and you're intelligent and we have things in common."

"Except the most important thing. Trust me on this one. I teach biology, remember." He studied her curiously. "Are you trying to talk yourself into being attracted to me? I'm flattered. Sort of. Although let me clue you in. Men don't enjoy being called *nice* any more than women do."

"But I always go for nice guys." With the notable exception of ex-Sergeant Jared Cain. However else she might describe him, *nice* was definitely not on the list. He was sexy. Intriguing. Hard-edged. Not nice. "Every real boyfriend I've ever had has been . . . you know. That word."

"Nice," he said with a sigh.

"What's wrong with that? Sensible people build a relationship on a foundation of affection and respect, not fantasy. Right?"

"Sometimes. Which is why I asked you out when we first met, what, two years ago? But there wasn't any spark. There has to at least be the potential for fantasy, if that's what you want to call it. Or some underlying chemistry. You didn't feel anything."

"I thought we were talking biology." She hesitated, wondering if she'd strayed into emotional quicksand trying to get David to help untangle her confused feelings about Jared Cain. "Do you mean that *you* felt—"

"Let's leave my feelings out of this," he said evenly.

For the first time in the discussion, Marnie could feel hot color run into her cheeks. Oh, damn, maybe David had wanted more from those dates than he'd sensed she was able to give. Maybe without intending it she'd hurt him—and was hurting him now by talking about this.

"There's a spark in you, Marnie," he continued. "You just need the right guy to build it into a fire."

Her hand touched the knob. "David, I—" What was there to say? "I seem to have embarrassed myself two days in a row."

"What's that mean?"

"Never mind. Are we still friends?"

His smile was the same as ever. "Of course."

JARED DUG THROUGH the printout that was folding itself into a neat stack as it spilled from the printer. He'd been waiting all day for the right time to call Marnie Rainbrook. Right off the bat in the morning would be too soon. Midmorning still would leave him looking overeager.

That was how he felt, though. For the first time in a long time, he was eager. Eager about a woman.

After finding the stock exchange prices he'd been searching for, he paused to get himself a cup of coffee, bitter and black the way he liked it. The slow drip of the coffeemaker reminded him of a clock's monotonous tick. Despite the self-deprecating things he'd said to Marnie yesterday, his workday was usually an excitement-filled blur, filled with talking, trading and stalling until the absolutely perfect moment to buy or sell went flitting across his computer screen. Today he'd been so distracted he'd had to sneak out to the printer used by the whole staff to get figures he should have picked up from the TV in his office, which was permanently tuned to a business channel.

That was it, he thought. Enough dodging the issue. He was going to call her. Now.

Heading purposefully into his office, he punched in the number of The Oaks with the hand that wasn't busy holding his mug. Looking it up was the first thing he'd had his secretary do when they'd both arrived in the predawn darkness. Chicago brokerage houses opened at the same time as New York firms. But what was an almost decent hour on the East Coast was an indecent hour earlier in the Midwest.

A receptionist answered with a brisk, "The Oaks. May I direct your call?"

"Marnie Rainbrook, please."

A click followed, and then a male voice said, "Hullo?"

A male voice? And a definitely informal one, at that.

"I'm trying to reach Marnie Rainbrook," Jared said, swishing his coffee thoughtfully. "Is she in?"

"You just missed her. The paint-ball war got a little out of hand and she's taking a shower."

A male voice that knew she was in the shower? Paint-something war? What kind of place was this, anyway?

Jared remembered the mug in his hand and sipped. Might as well find out what was going on. Marnie certainly hadn't indicated she was living with anyone.... "Who the hell are you?" he asked.

The voice sounded mildly taken aback. "I'm her office mate. I teach here. Who the hell are you?"

A STINGING HOT SHOWER restored some of Marnie's levelheadedness. David hadn't looked devastated. If anything, he'd talked to her like a big brother. After dressing in another simple blouse and pair of slacks, she wandered back to the office along a neatly gravelled path that began at the studio apartment The Oaks provided for her. As she came in, David waved a message slip at her.

"Somebody named Jared. I don't suppose he's the cause of all our soul-searching today, is he, ducks?"

Ignoring both the question and his amused tone, Marnie grabbed the paper. She leaned over her desk without bothering to sit in her swivel chair and punched buttons on the phone they shared. It was a slightly different number from the one on his card; she knew without having to look. She'd studied the card intently last night and had inadvertently memorized the number on it.

Perhaps not so inadvertently, she admitted to herself as a hollow ring sounded in her ear.

"Want me to leave?" David asked, looking very settled-in.

"Yes. Wait—no. It's just an answering machine." Her initial feeling of disappointment changed into a burst of pleasure at the sound of Jared Cain's voice. *This is crazy,* she thought. *The man's just repeating his number and telling you to wait for the beep.* But somehow Jared managed to sound sexy while he did it. How far gone could she be? She'd only met him yesterday for slightly less than an hour, for Pete's sake.

When it was her turn to speak, she said softly, "Hi, Sarge. This your private line? It's me—Marnie Rainbrook. I'm answering your call. I hate to play telephone tag with you, but I'm in right now and obviously you're not, so give me a call again when you can. I—I'd like to hear from you. Uh, goodbye."

Hanging up, she said, "I hate talking to machines. I can never think of anything brilliant to say."

"I doubt that'll be a problem when this Jared hears your recording."

"What's that mean?"

"It means, sweet Marnie, that from the lilt in your voice it sounds as if you've definitely found a match to light your fantasy."

"That's ridiculous."

He grinned.

"I mean, I didn't say anything . . . like that. Nothing that could be interpreted as—as—"

"A proposition," he said helpfully. "You didn't have to. It was the *way* you said it. Just watch out for your cute little, er, rear end. About the camp-out—who needs to work off some hormones—the boys or you?"

Marnie crumpled the message slip and threw it at him. It bounced off his nose.

"Back to the job we're getting paid for," she said firmly. "Frenchman's Lake would be the best choice, I think. The terrain's not as flat as it is around here, and there are some interesting hikes."

"Vertical hikes, you mean." He groaned for theatrical effect. "I suppose you'll want us all up on that crazy rope bridge of yours. Okay. We might as well get as much use out of the campground as we can before it's sold out from under us."

"It's not a sale, it's a trade, but I can't believe the board of trustees is really going through with it. That's the prettiest stretch of scenery imaginable. Brown County's as famous for its fall colors as New England."

"Do I detect a little Midwest chauvinism here?"

She made a face at him. "Almost as famous, anyway."

"It's not autumn. That land is also three hours away from The Oaks by car. The only reason the school owns it is because some patron of education donated it way back when. The property they want to swap for it is right next door. The campus will end up doubled in size. You can't blame the board, Marnie."

"Lots of the students do. They love going out there. It's so wild and free. Kids need a dose of wild and free every once in a while."

David pursed his lips. "Admit it, Marnie. So do you."

"Well, yeah, Frenchman's Lake is certainly one of my favorite places. When my family first sent me here, I was so lonely and so mixed-up. I mean, really mixed-up. Going out on survival camp-outs to the lake property helped me get my feet on the ground. Somehow the water, the sky and the trees showed me how to put my problems in perspective."

"That's not what I meant by wild and free."

Marnie stubbornly kept to the subject. "Anyway, the kids are afraid the new owners will want to clear-cut the woods. What does the forest service call it? Even-age management. That means after the trees are cut down, everything on the forest floor will be the same age. Dead."

David shrugged his bent shoulders. "Valuable timber in there. I suppose some people would call it good business."

Jared was a commodities broker. Did he deal in timber? Would he call destroying beauty business as usual?

"At least Kevin will get a chance to see the camp before the worst happens. If we waited for the regular fall trek and the land is swapped, he would miss out altogether. This extra trip will be a good thing. He's starting to take an active interest in his surroundings. I think he's actually beginning to open up."

"So you've been getting results? Good for you." David looked impressed. "The kid's still too cautious to say boo around me."

Marnie tilted her head. "I imagine it'll be one step forward, two steps back with that one. We were out on the tractor—he really *is* a wizard with mechanical things—and I thought everything was fine until I touched him. You know, just to point out something. He froze up."

"Froze," David repeated. "You sure his temperature didn't go in the other direction?"

"David! If I'd known asking you about a simple kiss would get you in this mood, I would have kept my big mouth shut. You've got sex on the brain."

"Most men between puberty and rigor mortis do," he murmured. "Kevin's the right age to develop a crush on a teacher. Especially an attractive female teacher less than ten years older than he is. A friendly adult's unthinking touch can be misconstrued by teenagers a lot more sophisticated than Kevin."

Marnie began to feel uneasy. "That's certainly true. But I didn't mean anything by it, David. I'll be more careful around him."

Nodding, David pushed back his chair. "Don't look so worried, honey. I'm probably way off-target. It's lunchtime. Come on; I'll treat you to a soda."

His suggestion reminded her of her own offer to buy Jared a beer yesterday. With a quick smile, she shook her head. "No, thanks. I'd better use the time to start organizing—if we're going out to Frenchman's Lake in the morning?" She said it as a question.

"Fine. I'll leave all that stuff to you."

After he had ambled out the door, Marnie got down on her hands and knees and scrambled around under David's desk until she found the crumpled bit of paper with Jared's private number. It was in the crevice between the desk wall and the wastepaper basket. She smoothed it out with careful fingers.

What if David was right, and she was like a bag of ready-to-light charcoal, waiting for the right spark? She considered the idea. A wild, flaming affair with Jared Cain?

She sank into a sitting position on the floor. The closest object was one of the easy chair's curved, uncomfortable legs, and she leaned against it.

Marnie Rainbrook wasn't the kind of woman who had affairs. She might occasionally wish she were, but the emptiness of casual sex was so clear to her that even in the midst of her teenage rebellion she'd known better than to go hopping from bed to bed. She dated and made male friends easily. When she reached twenty she had tried sleeping with one, and then another one, to see if friendship might ripen into something deeper, richer. It hadn't. Trying to force feelings that weren't there had killed both friendships. Since then, Marnie had gently put off any date who tried to take an aggressive step toward a sexual relationship.

She was older now. So why not? Why *not* a flaming love affair?

For one thing, if he calls again in the next few days, you're going to be gone, she reminded herself. Jared could just keep on phoning, she decided. After all, she'd risked the first advance; he owed her more than one call in return.

For another thing, she didn't believe in love at first sight. Or first phone call. They were barely acquaintances, not solid friends, she and this formidable near-stranger. His preferences and capabilities, sexual or otherwise, might be . . . anything.

Her whole mood, her edgy sense of anticipation, was built on nothing more than a short conversation, Jared's look at her legs—and her T-shirt—and David's interpretation of the tone of her voice.

Ridiculous.

Even if she'd managed to do something crazy like fall into instant infatuation with the smoky-voiced Sergeant Cain, it wasn't in her nature to act on an irresponsible and probably fleeting attack of hormones. She would take her students camping with David. They'd all have a couple of days of supervised excitement and achievement in the woods at Frenchman's Lake. And the sparkle and fizz in her veins would die down so she could figure out just how she felt about Jared Cain. If he called again, fine. If he didn't . . . she'd just have to live with it.

Folding the note into a neat square, she tucked it into her pocket, next to the business card she hadn't stopped carrying since yesterday. Love at first sight wasn't for her, she assured herself again.

5

SO MUCH FOR protecting your heart . . . and other parts of your anatomy, Marnie thought two days later. The man's going to think you're chasing him.

Jared's building was as tall and sleek as its neighbors along the glass-and-steel canyon of LaSalle Street. Marnie double-checked the number of the suite housing Cain and Marshall Associates against the card in her hand. Since it had been jostling inside her pocket for a couple of days, it was worn and a trifle grubby.

She felt grubby, too. Her jeans and hiking boots were more than appropriate for the woods, which was where she'd been until six hours ago, but the outfit was definitely out of place in a slick, urban setting. Little black suits were what these surroundings called for. Marnie fidgeted as she waited for the elevator. Trying to be unobtrusive, she knocked dirt and moss off her boots and onto the marble floor.

The elevator arrived. Sighing, she stepped into the cage. It rose with a silent speed that underscored the building's general feel of prosperity. The other passengers shifted to avoid contact with her, and she couldn't blame them. Although she'd washed up as best she could that morning, her clothes looked a little worse for wear. In contrast, the people around her were impeccably dressed. A perfume counter mix of feminine scents and men's colognes drifted from the others like a cloud. The place even smelled like money.

Her father would have approved, she thought vaguely.

Cain and Marshall took up the entire penthouse. Marnie straightened her shoulders. It was a good thing she'd left her less-than-stylish backpack in her van. Her appearance was out of place enough without that.

Inside the suite was an assortment of handsomely framed art and scattered antiques. The furnishings didn't exactly make Jared's place of work cozy, but they were certainly impressive. A decorative receptionist smiled while her heavily mascaraed eyes took in Marnie's appearance. The smile stayed valiantly in place. Marnie interpreted it with ease. You never knew what kind of eccentric exterior hid a bank account full of cash waiting to be invested.

"I'm here to see Jared Cain," said Marnie with an equally bright smile.

"Do you have an appointment?"

"Uh, no. But he knows me. Would you please tell him I'm here? My name is—"

"Mr. Cain is one of the partners, you know," the receptionist pointed out. Her smile had dimmed. "Perhaps a junior broker could help you instead?"

"I don't think so."

Marnie felt her confidence seep out of her. She'd driven to Chicago certain at some level too deep to be questioned that Jared would be willing to see her. Maybe her impetuous nature had really landed her in an embarrassing situation this time.

She put her nose in the air to conceal her uncertainty. The disappointment of being foiled in her effort to talk with the sexy Sergeant Cain hurt.

"Perhaps if I spoke to the office manager . . ." she suggested.

The receptionist sniffed and picked up a phone receiver. "I'll find out if Mrs. Harmon can speak to you."

Mrs. Harmon turned out to be a formidable-looking middle-aged woman.

"Yes?" said the older woman without warmth.

"Jared Cain," replied Marnie just as directly. "He asked me to get in touch with him. Is he in?"

Mrs. Harmon's small, dark eyes studied her. Marnie's untidy hair was scraped into a braid that tumbled over the shoulder of her plaid flannel shirt, and dried mud was crumbling from her boots onto the Oriental carpet.

"Your name, please?"

Marnie told her and was pleased to see some of the freezing composure crack. Perhaps Jared had mentioned her.

"I'll check Mr. Cain's schedule," said the other woman grudgingly. Figuring it would be a long wait, Marnie sat and contemplated the trail of Brown County dirt she'd left on Jared's lovely rug. She winced slightly. Her stepmother had such a carpet—hanging on a wall. Jared's looked just as old and valuable.

Mrs. Harmon returned almost instantly. "Mr. Cain will see you now." Under the cold correctness, Marnie detected a flare of curiosity.

"Thanks," she said breezily, as if she'd never had any doubt that Jared would be thrilled to see her, and followed the older woman through several other offices. The cubicles were simple and functional. She found herself relaxing. The world of business didn't attract her, but at least the part of Jared's firm where the real business was done wasn't ostentatious. The crackle of competing shouted conversations drowned out the click of fingers on keyboards and the hum of electronic equipment. It sounded like any busy workplace.

Then she tensed up all over again as Jared came through a door and walked toward her.

Days ago, he'd been a stalking tiger in baggy fatigues. Today his beautifully fitted suit of charcoal gray proclaimed him to be a successful hunter in a different but equally dangerous type of jungle. More than ever, Marnie was aware of her uncombed hair and how hopelessly inappropriate her clothes were.

"Hi," he said, stopping in front of her. He put out his hand. Somehow hers disappeared into it. It wasn't a business handshake; it was as warm as a hug, yet firm. She would have had to tug hard to pull her hand away.

Marnie looked up at him soberly. Her palm was dwarfed by his in a way that was reassuring and...erotic...at the same time. Love at first, or even second, sight was a myth, she repeated to herself. All too apparently, sheer sexual attraction was not. Her heart pounded. She had the terrible feeling the antiperspirant she'd smeared on herself—Lord, was it yesterday?—had failed abruptly. Jared smiled his half smile and her knees wobbled.

"Hi," she managed.

"Come into my office."

"Said the spider to the fly," she murmured under her breath. He didn't seem to hear. That was good. After all, she was the one trying to lure him into something. Just into giving some free advice. That wasn't so terrible, she tried to assure herself. *He doesn't handle other people's dirty odd jobs,* her conscience whispered.

Like the reception area, his office boasted an understated elegance. Jared noticed her quick appraisal. "Clients like knowing we make enough money to waste big chunks of it on the decor," he said, shrugging. "It reassures them."

"I bet." Marnie sat at one end of a long, low couch that was part of a conversational grouping near a window. Outside was a panoramic view of Lincoln Park. Pleasure and a subtle sense of danger combined to form a champagne fizz in her tummy when he sat next to her.

He laid an arm across the back of the couch. "What's the matter?" he asked calmly.

She sat back. A tingle ran along the nape of her neck at the awareness that his arm was a movement away. "Am I that obvious?"

"Well, yeah." He frowned. "Something brought you here in a hurry. And you had a glow the other day. It's gone. Can I help put it back?"

Her conscience went into overdrive. She was fairly sure he wasn't going to like the reason why she'd driven to Chicago to see him. "You're nice, did you know that, Sarge?"

Jared shook his head. Hell, did she have him pegged wrong. But he said, "So tell nice old Sarge what the problem is."

For a moment her face lit with laughter, and her head leaned back so it brushed his arm. He could feel the touch through his jacket and shirtsleeves. As if it were the most natural thing in the world, his arm slipped around her shoulders.

"I'll have to start calling you Slick," she said with a tiny gasp. "Does that 'nice old Sarge' line go over with most women?"

"You're the first one I've ever tried it on." She was the first one young enough to make him feel his age.

"I suppose it would be a tactical error to tell you it works."

"Depends on what you're trying to accomplish." This conversation was getting out of hand. So were his physical reactions to the lithe body lounging so trustingly against him. Life flowed through her—warmth, breath, pulse. She smelled earthy. Elementally woman. A wall away, computers hummed and televisions blared the latest market prices. People did business. His business. All of it had never seemed so far away.

Jared shifted, raising one ankle to rest on the opposite knee and adjusting his jacket in the hope that his actions would hide how hard and fast his body had responded to hers. This was the second time he'd been near her, and the second time her presence had caused his arousal to flare with the instant, overwhelming potency of a randy teenager's.

He had to do something about this. Either get her into bed—fast—or get out of her trusting orbit. It had been years since he'd rushed a woman into sex before he thought both of them were ready to play. Marnie wasn't a toy. Marnie was . . . she was getting under his skin, that's what she was doing.

"So what's the problem, honeybun?" The silly endearment just slipped out. His voice was hoarse, and he cleared his throat. In an automatic gesture, he dug into his shirt pocket for cigarettes.

But his motion had drawn her gaze downward—to her jeans, not his. She exclaimed in disgust, "Oh, Jared, look what I'm doing to your beautiful office. Your cleaning people will have a fit over all this mud."

"They're paid to clean," he said without much interest as he snapped his lighter. The decorator touches were for the clients, not for him. He would have been just as happy with a desk, a phone, a computer terminal and nothing else. "Paid well, too. Maybe they'll enjoy the challenge. Marnie, are you going to tell me what's going on?"

She took a deep breath. "I need you."

He lifted his chin and regarded the ceiling. The smoke from the first bitter-tasting drag curled in a lazy pattern high up in the air. Did she *know* how she affected him? Was she teasing him sexually? No, he decided, risking a swift glance at her earnest expression. Marnie wasn't a tease.

"So, what do you need me to do?" he asked the ceiling.

"Give me some advice. The stuff you used to do for the army—what do you call it?"

"Emergency ordinance disposal." Whatever he'd been expecting, this wasn't it. His concentration had been splintered between a male awareness of Marnie and his need to control it. Now he focused sharply on her unbusinesslike clothing and the look of strain around her eyes. In spite of a flinch he couldn't quite suppress, he asked, "You run across a bomb you need disposed of, lady?"

"Lord, I hope not. I'm sorry to bring you this problem, Jared. You said you don't mess with stuff like this—"

He waved away her apology. "Just tell me, okay?"

"One of the other teachers and I had some students out in the woods with us the last few days. The campground and surrounding area were booby-trapped. Trees were spiked and wires had been stretched across paths to trip hikers." She shook her head at the memory. "I couldn't believe it. I've taken groups out there dozens of times. It's one of the loveliest, most serene places in the world. This—this was like a desecration."

With a stab, Jared mashed his cigarette in the ash-tray that Mrs. Harmon made sure was always in precisely the same spot on the teak coffee table. "Scary, huh?"

"It was so unexpected," she explained. "I was responsible for bringing those kids out there. I mean, yes, I'm supposed to be teaching them survival skills, but—"

"You what?"

"I teach survival skills. It's part of the philosophy of our school. But nobody thought there'd be so much to have to survive. I don't mind admitting this isn't the sort of situation I'm trained to handle. Am I making any sense?"

She raised her head. There were a remarkable number of emotions in her expressive eyes. Caution and trust. Hesitant pleasure and trust. Remembered fear and trust.

Trust.

"Sort of. Survival skills, huh? Like living off tree bark and berries and stuff like that?"

Some of the trust faded. "I won't talk about it if you're going to laugh at me."

"I'm not laughing." He'd rarely found an idea less amusing.

"Good." She inspected him a moment more, then amplified, "Part of my job is to construct situations that allow the kids to overcome obstacles. I don't do anything regular teachers don't do, I just do it in a different way. I help students achieve and gain confidence in themselves. By the time they graduate, they know a little woodcraft, a smidgeon of karate, some basic mechanical skills." Marnie shrugged. "The one thing I can't pump into them is common sense. I hope it comes along with growing up."

He wouldn't touch that comment with a pole considerably longer than ten feet. So far, common sense didn't seem to be her strong point. "Tree-spiking sounds like environmental terrorists. Would some kooky organization have a reason to target these woods you're talking about?"

A breath puffed out her cheeks before she let it escape through her lips. "It's just a little, private stretch of forest in the hill country. The only towns nearby have names like Beanblossom and Gnaw Bone. An old student left the property to The Oaks. There's been some talk about selling it, but that wouldn't be of general interest to radical environmental groups. It's not the only home of an endangered species or anything. A lot of Oaks students and alumni are bothered by the possibility the trees might be cut down by the new owners. Still, no reasonable person would go to the extent of planting booby traps to save it."

"Reasonable people don't drive huge nails into trees or lay trip wires under any circumstances," he pointed out. "Do you know what spikes can do when they're struck by chain saws?"

She winced. "Kill the logger holding the chain saw."

"Right. This is really a matter for the police. Hold on a minute; let me make a call."

"Don't say where this is happening," she said quickly.

"I won't." Striding to his desk, he picked up the phone. After a terse conversation, he hung up and came back to the sofa, stretching his arm around her in another protective cuddle. "Guy I know at the forest service. He says at the least the culprits ought to be fined. It could mean jail—and if somebody gets hurt it would be a felony conviction."

"Oh, I doubt the school would want anybody official called in," she said with a vagueness he didn't like at all.

His hand tightened on her shoulder. "Marnie, this isn't anything to fool around with. Creeps who set traps for other human beings ought to be in jail. You have reported this to your bosses, haven't you?"

"Oh, sure. David—you talked to him on the phone a couple of days ago—David's going to tell the headmaster. But I thought there'd be something I could do. I love those woods, Jared. I know them better than the palm of my hand. Surely there's some action I—"

Skepticism thinned his mouth as he assessed her light bones and slim figure. "Leave it to the authorities. Will this David be able to describe exactly what you saw?"

"Of course." Nothing but simple surprise colored her tone. "He was there, too."

"Sleeping with you?" His tone was carefully neutral.

Marnie flushed. "At the campground, yes. With me, no. We were chaperoning a group of teenagers. Jared, do you think I'd go hopping from sleeping bag to sleeping bag on a trip that included a bunch of kids? Kids in my care?"

Obeying instinct, his fingertips brushed her fine-grained cheek. The skin felt hot because of the blush and soft because—because it was Marnie's skin, he supposed. "No. I don't think you'd do that."

"Gee, thanks." Edginess still crackled between them, but he noted she wasn't moving away. She even raised her face so that her cheek rubbed against his fingers. "For the record, David is a friend of mine and he wouldn't flaunt a relationship like that in front of the students, either. If we had that kind of relationship. Which we don't, and never have."

Her voice had gradually softened, and now her eyes met his. It wasn't hard to read the question in them.

He put it into words for her. "Are we going to have a relationship?" he asked quietly.

A discreet cough jerked his head around.

Marnie jumped slightly. Released from his compelling gaze, she looked toward the door he'd never closed.

"Mr. Cain?" Another well-groomed woman stood there. Marnie wondered how many more impeccably dressed females were lurking around Jared's offices. She felt dowdier than ever. The woman went on, "Your reservation is confirmed for seven this evening."

The secretary named a trendy restaurant Marnie recognized by reputation. It was highly rated by food critics and extremely pricey.

"Thanks, Noelle," Jared said, not looking away from Marnie. "That okay with you, Ms. Rainbrook?"

"Sounds fine, Mr. Cain."

Was she just possibly saying yes to more than dinner? Belated caution came to her rescue. Pitching her protest quietly, so the secretary couldn't hear, she murmured, "Maybe next time, though, you could ask first."

"Message received." Out loud, he said, "Tell Mr. Marshall I'm leaving now, will you, Noelle?"

The secretary withdrew, and Jared ran the tips of his fingers across her skin again, this time along her throat. It burned where he touched. "Am I making a false assumption here? You'll need to tell me if I am, honeybun. The politest way to explain how I'm feeling is that I'm very, very attracted to you. If you don't feel the same way or I'm moving too fast, say so."

Marnie flicked a piece of dried moss from her jeans. "If I said that was the case, what would you do?"

"My damnedest to change your mind," he answered promptly.

She still didn't understand the hot-and-cold conversation they'd had in Liberty Hollow, but his directness now pleased her. "I imagine your damnedest would be a lot of fun, but it's not necessary," she said, just as straightforwardly. "I'm attracted, too."

"I like your style."

She shrugged, wondering why she felt shy all of a sudden. "I guess I'm just not very good at game playing between men and women. Maybe I should try being mysterious or hard-to-get or something."

"Marnie." His hand was warm and comforting as it massaged the base of her neck. "I said I like the way you are. Keep in mind, though, that openness and honesty aren't very effective survival instincts. You're too trusting."

Marnie burst into laughter. "Come on, Sarge. We both know I'm secure with you."

"I'm the last man in the world you'll ever be safe with, Marnie Rainbrook. Don't forget that."

His flat, pleasant tone rattled her. But then he was snapping the Off switch on his personal computer and grabbing her hand to lead her out of the office.

"I can wait around if you have to finish up anything here at the office—"

"As a rule, I don't usually pick up and walk out," he admitted with a crooked smile. "But you're worth breaking a few rules for."

His fingers intertwined with hers on the ride in the elevator to the basement parking garage where his gleaming foreign car was parked.

Once in the car, Marnie didn't ask where they were going. She simply relaxed into the supple leather upholstery and let herself enjoy the spacious car, and the big man next to her.

After uncounted minutes of sliding smoothly through the heavy Chicago traffic, she said, "We should stop at a car wash to get me hosed down before you take me anywhere."

For once he looked startled. "I wasn't even thinking. Do you want to change? Are there any clothes in your car? In fact, do you have a car?"

"A van. It's parked near your office building. There aren't any clothes in it, though. Where are we?" She glanced out the window. "Near the Magnificent Mile? I see a department store. Unless you've got something else planned before the reservation time at the restaurant, I can transform myself."

The store she'd spotted happened to belong to one of the most expensive chains in the country. Taking in her untroubled expression, Jared figured she didn't know that. Well, it wasn't a problem. He had a couple of credit cards on him.

"WHAT DO YOU LIKE?" she asked, raising her eyebrows at him over a rack of blouses, not one of which cost less than three hundred dollars.

There was a lacy shell that would reveal more than it hid. Jared appreciatively decided it would be worth the money to see that cobweb of lace defining Marnie's peaked breasts. He gave the shell serious consideration until he remembered which restaurant they were going to. It was an elegant place with a wonderful menu and he hoped Marnie would like it. Unfortunately, the service was so stately it bordered on slow. Jared was fairly sure his blood pressure—not to mention the pressure on another part of his body—wouldn't be able to cope with the sight of Marnie in that particular blouse for hours on end.

"Dinner," he said, inspired. "That means a dress, right?"

"Okay."

She seemed willing to go along with whatever he said. Willing. Damn, he wanted her willing.

Her braid swinging, she pivoted and pointed to another rack, where garments shimmered in a rainbow of party fabrics. He saw a color that reminded him of her eyes and grabbed a swatch of skirt. "This."

The opalescent gray glowed in his large hands. Marnie hid a smile. "That's a size sixteen," she said gently. "But it gives me an idea what to shoot for. Okay, Sarge, scram."

"What?"

"Go get yourself a cup of espresso, or hang around the escalators and stare at the pretty girls or something. I'll be ready for you in an hour." She glanced at her watch. "That'll make it six-thirty. Is the time all right?"

"Sure." He could always settle the bill for her then. "Meet you here?"

She agreed with a smile, and continued to smile as he left with his prowling stride, his tall male figure a handsome and alien sight among the aisles crowded with feminine things. Then she turned to a saleslady. She had a lot to do.

"First of all," Marnie said, "is the buyer for this department or a personal shopper still on duty?"

The saleslady admitted that the personal shopper was working late.

"Great. Please see if she can help me. And I'm desperately in need of a wash and style within the next hour. Would you check with the salon . . ."

There weren't many customers at this quiet hour, after the afternoon crowds and before the nighttime influx of bored teenagers. Marnie wasn't sure if the flurry of attention she received was due to a lag in business or to her imitation of her stepmother's most regal manner. At any rate, her woodsy clothes didn't seem to count against her. The personal shopper jumped to fill her requests. And the stylist who was free in the beauty salon went to work on her hair with gum-snapping enthusiasm.

By the time the personal shopper was draping the loose collar of an evening tunic around her neck so that it fell off one of her shoulders, Marnie was confident of her presentability.

The tunic was made of silk. It looked and felt like sin. The silver color streamed over her slight curves with the softness of moonlight. From under the classic tunic peeked a mere inch of skirt. An exotic belt of more silk—scarlet this time—bound her waist. Twists of red-enamelled metal dangled from her ears when she turned her head this way and that in the dressing room mirror. During the previous half hour, while the salon had slaved over her, the personal shopper had found tiny scraps of silver evening slippers in her size. Marnie tied the thin straps—they were spun of actual silver wires and had diamond chips at the ends—and picked up the miniscule matching purse.

"Girl, you'll knock this guy dead," said the woman frankly.

"Oh, I don't want him dead," murmured Marnie, feeling half scared and half wicked. She took a deep breath. "I guess this is it, huh?"

The personal shopper swept back the curtain with a flourish. Marnie's nerves were unaccountably shaken by the sight of herself looking sleek and glamorous in clothes with one purpose. To attract Jared Cain. The woman's dramatic gesture made her laugh nervously, and she stepped out onto the showroom floor.

Jared would have recognized Marnie if she'd been wearing a paper sack. But as she glided into the light in a filmy thing that made her look as if she were naked under a thin coating of moonbeams, he had a brief, disorienting vision of her in flannel shirt and jeans.

"What happened to the moss in your braid?" He hadn't meant his voice to be hoarse. It was.

She ran her fingers through the blond waterfall of hair cascading down her back. It had been crimped and pulled up into a loose and fancy ponytail. "Do you miss it?"

He was confused. "What?"

"The moss."

He did miss it, a little. She'd turned him on in muddy forest gear. But now she looked like sex incarnate. Jared dragged a hand through his own hair, wondering how the hell he was supposed to eat when what he really wanted was to strip Marnie of her moonbeams and— he cut his thoughts off there. They would only add to his problems.

The silk defined her smoothly muscled body like water. Something like reverence came to his aid by distracting him from his raw physical reaction. She was so full of life.

Jared watched her chew on a bottom lip painted a rich, luscious red. He forgot to think at all.

"Aren't we going to dinner?" she asked uncertainly.

He shook his head, trying to force intelligence back into it. "Yeah. You ready?"

"All except for paying the piper." She held out her hand for a bill the saleslady was quick to pass to her.

"I'll handle that." Jared reached over and plucked the paper from her hand. He glanced at it and began to pull his wallet from his back pocket.

"Jared? What are you doing?"

Her shocked voice made him self-conscious. "You got all duded-up because I chose a restaurant that isn't the corner diner. My choice, my bill."

"And you're perfectly welcome to take care of the check for the food," she said hotly. "But I'm not a child who needs somebody to buy my clothes for me. And in case you're wondering, I'm not a...a..." She seemed to fish for the right word. "I'm not a bimbo, either."

"I never—"

Marnie marched to the counter. Her tiny purse swung defiantly at the end of its extravagantly long shoulder strap. "Would you check in the computer for me? Look under Rainbrook. There ought to be an account in my name."

"Yes, miss. Er, ma'am." The clerk obviously was having difficulty deciding how Marnie ought to be addressed. Jared doubted any woman, young or old, really wanted to be called *ma'am*. Just as obviously, Marnie was too flamingly angry to care.

"Rainbrook, Marnie. Is that the correct listing? Yes, ma'am, you have an account. The limit is—"

"Look, Marnie, I didn't mean to insult you," Jared murmured. He came up behind her quietly, using the same caution he'd show if he were approaching a grenade. His instinct was to touch her. Before his career in the army had literally blown up in his face, he'd loved handling danger, thrived on the contact with raw energy controlled by his own hands. And right now, Marnie Rainbrook was dangerous.

"The limit is . . . there is no limit," the clerk said.

Jared's head swivelled. "That's unheard of for a store account."

The clerk was blinking at the screen. "You're right, sir, it is. But that's what the records show. Shall I put the bill on your account, Ms. Rainbrook?"

"Absolutely not." Marnie dug a checkbook out of the ridiculously small purse, which was barely large enough to hold it. "I'll pay. I assume my personal check is good here?"

"Yes, ma'am," the clerk assured her fervently.

"Feisty, aren't you?" said Jared. He gave in to compulsion and touched the end of one scarlet earring. It spun, and his fingers grazed the side of her neck. A sizzle of sexual awareness ran through the pads of his fingers. He could tell she felt it, too, by the way her shoulders swayed restlessly, but she didn't move away. "If you don't believe in using credit, why have an account?" he asked.

She didn't look up from scribbling her signature across a check. *Damn, damn, damn.* This grand gesture was going to wipe out most of the reserve she had in the bank. Until Jared had behaved as if they were characters in the kind of movie where a rich, handsome prince buys up Rodeo Drive for an immoral Cinderella, she'd accepted the plundering of her checking account as worth it. This was what she got for chasing him all the way to Chicago. She might deserve it, but she didn't have to like it.

Marnie shot him a sideways glance. Even if—maybe especially if—she'd laid her pride open to Jared's mistaken assumption, her anger was still burning hot and it was all directed at the man tickling her neck.

"My father opened this line of credit for me. He's got department store charge cards for me all over town. It just so happens I prefer to pay my own way. However, you can rest assured I've already got a daddy. I don't need another one. Particularly not a sugar daddy. Got it?"

He set her other earring spinning. "Got it. Ready to eat now?"

She was suddenly starving. "Yes, thank you."

"Okay, let's go." His grin was lopsided, and far too attractive.

The clerk lifted a bag from behind the counter. Marnie knew it contained the soiled things she'd brought with her. "Shall I throw this away?" the woman asked, wrinkling her nose.

"Certainly not," said Marnie haughtily. She took it and clutched it to her as if it contained priceless gems. "These are my very best hiking boots." The earrings swung wide as she turned to Jared. "Okay," she echoed, "let's go."

6

"SO WHEN DID YOU LEARN to be so damned independent about money?" Jared asked around a mouthful of raw oyster.

Marnie regarded the gray, wobbly objects, served in their natural mother-of-pearl settings. *No*, she told herself. This was one challenge she was going to ignore. "About the time I realized allowing somebody else to support me meant I was giving up control of my own life. When did you learn to swallow shooters?"

"In Nam. You could order 'em in a shot of booze. There are bars that serve them like that here in the States, too."

"Ick."

He grinned. "Who was trying to smother you in luxury?" The grin faded. "An ex-husband? Ex-boyfriend?"

"Neither. My father and stepmother."

Jared relaxed. "Was that such a bad deal?" he asked lazily.

The amber bubbles in her champagne cocktail rose to the top of the fluted goblet. She watched them, and then said, "Can we talk about this without you coming to the conclusion I'm still in the cradle?"

"With you in that dress?" He snorted softly. "Don't worry, I won't make that mistake."

Not quite sure she believed him, Marnie began, "I was what you might call a problem adolescent. If you wanted to be polite. Father and my stepmother tried to bribe me out of my rebellious stage. Unfortunately, that just turned me from a problem adolescent into a spoiled adolescent."

Lifting the last of the oysters, he said, "I find it hard to believe you were ever anything but a joy to be with."

She toyed with the stem of her goblet. "I didn't take well to my father's remarriage. Like a lot of kids, I saw the appearance of a replacement parent as an act of betrayal on my father's part. That's even though my mom had died the year before. The funny thing is, one of the reasons he married Louisa was because he saw me floundering in my grief and he thought I needed a mother."

"But Louisa wasn't it."

"Lord, no. She tried. She bullied Father into taking me out of a public junior high school and putting me into an elite private school instead. And she painted my room pink—I hate pink—and she taught me how to shop. That's how I got gorgeous for you on an hour's notice." Highlights dazzled him as Marnie flicked a red-tipped finger through the ends of her hair. "So I guess not all her efforts to turn me into a fifties-style debutante were wasted. Nobody was more surprised than she was when the well-brought-up daughters of her terribly well-bred friends recruited me into their idea of fun and games."

"Wild parties?" Jared guessed.

"Very wild. And shoplifting." The tart aftertaste of the cocktail lingered on her tongue. It wasn't any more bitter than the memory of that artificial, unhappy year when she'd been thirteen-going-on-thirty. The sick panic that had wrenched her stomach the times she'd allowed herself to be taunted into stealing was an emotion she never wanted to feel again. She sipped her fizzy drink. "Father and Louisa imagined I'd stop stealing if I had accounts everywhere."

"Did their cure work?"

She hummed a snatch of an old Beatles tune. Jared recognized "Can't Buy Me Love." Moving her goblet out of the way so the waiter could set a salad before her, she added, "They thought it did. Actually, I was glad of the excuse to stop. Shoplifting terrified me. I felt so guilty afterward I always mailed the items back. But I'd discovered the wonderful power to make the two of them notice me. On my terms, not theirs. I started a campaign of attention-getting behavior. The dressing on this salad is fantastic. How's your soup?"

Jared remembered to taste it. "Great. Did you succeed in getting their attention?"

"You bet. I ran away. To Greece."

He choked. A waiter materialized to pat him on the back, or perform the Heimlich maneuver, but Jared glared the man away.

"Greece?"

"Uh-huh. I'd read this book—*My Brother Michael*, by Mary Stewart—and decided I was going to find my destiny in Delphi. That's a tourist spot with lots of ruins and atmosphere."

"Did you? Find your destiny?"

"I only got as far as the Athens airport. Father had people from the American embassy waiting to turn me around and send me home. I never even got to the Parthenon, let alone the temple where the old Delphic Oracle used to tell fortunes. My career as a beautiful and tragic expatriate moping around Delphi was over before it began."

Jared was fascinated. "Then what?"

"What do you think?" She smiled at him with a touch of mischief. Her poise and assurance had him half believing she was kidding him along for some incomprehensible female reason.

"I think if your parents had had any sense they would have paddled you till you couldn't sit down and grounded you until graduation. *College* graduation," he growled.

Her crow of laughter drew stares from other diners. Jared noticed the men were giving her narrow-eyed once-overs, while the women studied her gown with frank envy. "You would make a great parent," she said appreciatively. "Unfortunately, they sent me to a shrink instead."

"That didn't help, either?"

"It might have, if any of us had been willing to listen to her. As it was, the shrink kept trying to get me to see I wasn't doing myself any good, and at that point I just didn't care. She worked to get Father and Louisa to understand I was after love, not the junk I'd stolen or exotic vacations. They didn't believe her."

"Why not?"

"They did love me. It was just that they didn't know how to show it, and I didn't know how to accept it. We're on better terms now. I visit them for holidays and birthdays. Louisa directs the conversations and plans the activities and I put a time limit on how long I stay. We smile a lot and never say anything important. It saves wear and tear on all our nerves."

"Poor little Marnie." He pushed the bowl away. Marnie's story was more interesting than the chef's creation. "So spill it. What *did* straighten you out?"

With her fork, she chased a morsel of *radicchio* around her plate. Catching the bit of purple lettuce, she popped it into her mouth. Jared watched her scarlet lips. "This is all a long time ago." When he waited patiently, she sighed and said, "The Oaks did the trick. I was sent there as a last resort."

"To learn how to boil bark and eat it."

"Don't tempt me into throwing something at you, Jared Cain. Imagine how embarrassing it would be to get tossed out of a ritzy place like this on our ears. For your information, The Oaks is highly regarded by experts who work with troubled youth."

He still couldn't envision her at a raucous teenage party or in a chronic state of anger at her family. "I know that," he said, nodding at the waiter who hovered over his soup plate.

The tilt of her head brought one of her earrings forward to rest against the curve of her jaw. "You know?"

"Ted Marshall," he explained. "He's got a brother-in-law in education. Looked up your Oaks for me. Said it has quite a reputation."

"You went to the trouble of finding out about The Oaks?" Marnie asked.

Shrugging, Jared replied, "It sounded different, that's for sure. I knew I wasn't going to see you right away, so it was a way to pass the time until I got to talk to you again."

The flames from three candles set in an asymmetrical arrangement between them illuminated Marnie's absorbed features. She understood what he was saying, he was sure of it. *I've been thinking about you, Marnie Rainbrook. A lot.*

She retreated into the depths of her chair. The wash of candlelight couldn't reach that far. Soft shadows hid her expression.

After a charged silence, she stirred and said, "It's a real school. Our graduates leave with a high school diploma, and plenty of them go on to college. Very few end up on drugs, on the street, in prison or in a morgue—which is where all of them are headed when they get sent to The Oaks."

Her tone was earnest but light. Jared wondered if he'd overwhelmed her. Subtly, she'd withdrawn from the intensity that pulsed between them like the rhythmical music pouring out of the lounge.

Obviously, her work took a prominent place in her life. Talking about a kid named Kevin, she leaned forward, and her gray eyes glowed with zeal. Silk-clad elbows ended up propped on the table. Her slim hands made extravagant gestures as she talked about the importance of a simple hug.

Bursts of a jazz number showered over them in tantalizing snatches of sound. Embarrassed at the way she'd run on about her work, Marnie let her shoulders move sinuously in time to the music. Jared had listened intelligently, asking questions and making comments that kept her talking far too long. Usually she could lose herself in a discussion of her kids. This time a prickly awareness of the man she was with kept interfering. She felt . . . she wasn't certain how she felt. Hot, boneless. A little reckless; a little scared.

She wanted Jared with an immediacy that should have shocked her. Only she wasn't shocked at all. Excitement drove the hard, fast pounding of her heart. Her nerve endings tingled under her growing sense of determination. Jared was going to be her lover. At least, he was going to be if there was anything she could do to make it happen.

She kept her voice calm. "So, you see, by providing an outlet for the kids' energy and creating situations that make it possible for them to succeed, the school helps them put their personal problems in perspective. The graduates will have learned methods of dealing with the real world that aren't self-destructive. They just go out and do whatever they have to do."

"Like drive a couple of hundred miles to get advice about booby traps," Jared suggested.

"Sure." The music had changed to a ballad, and she swayed to the beat.

"Want to take some of that can-do spirit onto the dance floor? It'll be a while before the entrées show up."

A crease appeared between her brows. "Was there a dance floor in the lounge? I can't remember."

"Do you care if there is or not?" he asked softly. "We can make our own space. I want to dance with you."

There was a dare in his eyes. Marnie put her hand in his outstretched palm and went with him to the lounge.

A round space about the size of a quarter had been provided near the stage where the band played. They slow-danced to the ballad. Then they slow-danced to a jumping, rock-inspired number. All this power in my hands, she thought, sliding them across his shoulders. Muscles tensed under her light exploration. Hard muscles, under which were hard bones.

His gaze followed her movements as she brushed against him. It was erotic to feel him watching her. He wound his arms around her waist, and their legs tangled as if they were making love. Marnie finally stopped trying to move her feet at all, and put her arms around Jared's neck, letting her breasts crush against his chest and her hips rub his in a languid side-to-side motion.

She couldn't breathe, and around them the atmosphere was hot. Very hot.

"Enough of that now," he muttered under his breath. He pulled his arms away so abruptly that she almost melted to the floor at his feet. Then he reached for her hand and towed her back to the dining area.

The entrées had arrived. Digging into a platter of pasta and more shellfish, he ate with silent concentration. Marnie followed his example. She hadn't expected to be able to taste anything, but to her faint surprise she'd never experienced chicken so tender, or curry sauce so fiery and sweet. All her senses sprang to life around this man.

"Where'd you learn to do that?" he asked finally.

Marnie hefted a forkful of some exotic type of squash. "Chew and swallow?"

"Don't get funny, honeybun. I mean, where'd you learn to dance like that? If you call it dancing."

He sounded serious. She rested her fork at the side of her plate. "Are you asking me how many men there have been?"

Although colors were muted in the candlelight, she could see his cheeks darken. "I suppose I am. Forget it. None of my business." He skewered a prawn with a vicious stab.

"Not unless I want it to be," she agreed, and took a deep breath. "There was some drunken groping at those parties back when I was really messed up. More than making out, less than enough to get me pregnant. I was that smart, even if I was just thirteen. So, technically, I guess I was a virgin. A long time later I decided love was nothing more than a strong degree of like, and I had a couple of boyfriends I liked very much. One at a time, not both together," she added hastily. Jared had abandoned his prawns and his eyes never left her face.

"Oh, Marnie." She didn't know why he reached across the candles and ran a gentle thumb over her cheek until he held the finger out so she could see it. The tip was wet.

"Oh, God, am I crying?" She laughed shakily. "I never cry, honest."

"Maybe you ought to now and then." His gravelly voice was gentle, too.

Blotting the tears carefully with her napkin so she wouldn't ruin her makeup, she said firmly, "Tears aren't a cure for anything. None of this was tragic. Really. The choices were all mine. I suffered fewer consequences than I deserved, probably. Those guys were perfectly nice. It was just that sparks weren't there." She thought of David. Her fellow teacher had known what he was talking about. The spark was there with Jared. In fact, he *was* the spark. A dangerous man, she reminded herself.

"It is possible to have successful sex based on mild affection. But you don't seem like a we're-just-friends-who-happen-to-sleep-together-occasionally kind of woman."

"No, I'm not," she replied sincerely. Then a little smile played over her face. "At least not in practice. I admit to the occasional fantasy, though. I think most women fantasize a little. But, of course, fantasies don't pan out. Making love under water isn't very practical."

Jared grinned. "Too bad."

"Yeah," said Marnie, a little wistfully. "You can be pretty sure that the kind of guy who breaks into your bedroom in a fantasy won't turn out to be Prince

Charming in reality. Though, from what I've heard, that's a really common one."

"You're kidding."

"Not at all. But I learned the hard way, that fantasies have no place in the real world. I was lonely and I thought I could make friends into lovers."

The side of his mouth twitched. "I take it sleeping with guys you weren't in love with wasn't romantic?"

Trust Jared to see straight through her, she thought. Did he have to strip that younger Marnie's desire for romance bare? She glared straight into his eyes. "As a matter of fact, it wasn't. Look, can we change the subject?"

He ignored her demand. "Tried it since?"

"No."

Picking up a prawn by the tail, he ate it with relish. "Thinking of trying it again?"

"What are you asking? Whether or not I plan to say yes if you ever get around to suggesting I spend the night with you?" she asked heatedly. "Right this minute I'm not feeling very friendly!"

He pitched a bit of shell from the tail onto his plate. "That's a promising start." With a flick of his fingers, he called over the waiter. "Check."

"No dessert, sir?"

"We have other plans."

As he swept Marnie out of the restaurant, rebellion flickered in her. "You're taking things for granted again, Sarge."

"All you have to do is say no," he told her calmly. Whatever had disturbed his self-possession before was gone. He was maddeningly, attractively cool.

Then he spun her around to face him. Light from the doorway spilled all around them on the sidewalk. Wind poured in from Lake Michigan, lifting his hair and ruffling the collar of his jacket. He suddenly looked tough, a little grim, not cool at all. A jungle cat. An aroused one.

"I'm not some pimply teenager who thinks it'll fall off if you stop him before he's scored." It was simply the most direct way of saying what he meant. "And don't mistake me for some 'friend' who'll drop you if the first time doesn't result in fireworks, either. And God help us both if you think I'm some sensitive soul who can't take a rejection. When you want to say no, say no, damn it!"

How did he know how disappointing, how—how nothing those failed forays into intimacy had been? "Yes, sir, Sarge."

His big hands flexed on her upper arms. "I mean it, Marnie. I don't require any virgin—oh, all right, almost virgin—sacrifices. We go into this because we both want it, or we don't go into it at all."

"You make starting a relationship sound like a business deal." The pressure on her arms eased, and she realized she'd disconcerted him. The knowledge made her braver. She'd intended to speak wryly, but the next sentence came out soft and breathless. "I don't think a lack of fireworks will be a problem."

His hands became caressing. "You know what, Marnie Rainbrook? I'm glad you stopped sleeping with friends before I met you. Because I'm damned if all I want is to be your friend."

7

THE BOAT'S DECK swayed to the whistling of the wind. On the water it was always obvious why Chicago was called the Windy City. Marnie studied the oak parquet that glistened as brightly as her silver evening slippers and the teak fittings that hugged the walls of the trim cabin in Jared's miniyacht.

"Tell me again how you aren't interested in material things," she said, accepting the glass he was handing her.

His lips twisted ruefully. "I never said that. All I said was that we should come here instead of my place because the apartment's a dump."

She sipped. The port was a dignified relic from a bygone, gracious age. "I like this." She sipped again, and studied the dark puddle remaining at the bottom of the tiny wineglass. Was she hoping for a little false courage? Carefully, she set the glass down on a bentwood table with modern lines. "The port that underpaid teachers can afford generally tastes like educated prune juice."

"Would you like more?" He jiggled the decanter invitingly.

"No, thanks. Really, Jared, considering your car, your clothes, your boat and your booze, I find it hard to believe your apartment wouldn't be a showplace."

"All it has in it are a bed, a kitchen and a computer. I don't need much more. The firm uses the boat for entertaining," he said, putting down the decanter and sitting next to her.

With a finger on her shoulder, he turned her so her back fit into the curve of his body. It was simple instinct to cuddle as close as she could to his strength and warmth. She did, but the scared feeling inside her snapped into tense alertness, as it had more than once at the restaurant. This wasn't a fantasy.

"Doesn't that bother you?" The Grecian knot holding her ponytail was pressing uncomfortably against his breastbone. Before she could answer, his fingers became busy loosening it so that the honey blond hair sifted over his hands and wrists, and down her shoulders. It pooled in both their laps. He smoothed it softly from her forehead.

Marnie closed her eyes. A tiny, interrogative sound escaped her throat. Then she turned to face him and he was kissing her, and she made another startled noise. Sexy, dangerous, potent...his lips played over hers, and she clutched at him as if she were drowning. She *was* drowning. In sensation.

She'd had her share of kisses. They'd ranged from blah to mildly pleasurable to hot and desperate. There had been kisses that tasted like toothpaste, kisses from experts and kisses that had been marred by too much tongue or too many teeth. And kisses from men she'd been trying to fall in love with.

Jared kissed with a single-minded concentration that demanded total surrender. Her thoughts stopped. There was only the sound of their breathing and the frantic pounding of her heart in her chest. And his lips, rubbing their feel and their taste into her mouth, making her understand her own softness and vulnerability.

"Sweet," he muttered. "You're so sweet and trusting. God, you scare me to death."

Marnie's thinking processes started again with a jerk. They'd been short-circuited by the jolt from Jared's first kiss, and now they lurched along like the second hand of a clock that had forgotten how to tick.

She scared *him* to death? He *terrified* her. Jared made her feel soft, malleable. She wanted to be whatever he desired her to be. Very violently, she wanted his hands on her, molding her. But independence was important to her. If she gave away all that she was, would there be anything left?

Just then his palms moved down her back in a long glide that ended at her bottom. The sleek material of her tunic gathered and slithered under his touch. He palmed light circles into her firm buttocks, and every muscle she had flexed in response.

Marnie parted her lips to say something, but her brain clicked off again, so she kissed him instead—on his broad chest, on the cleft in his chin, on the mouth. The openmouthed kiss was an invitation for his tongue. He took it. She felt he was taking her, although there was so much still to come, to look forward to....

The dark invasion of his tongue sparked light behind her eyelids. Pinpoints of light that spun. If this was the result of his kisses, what would happen when his body made itself part of hers?

With a gasp, she pushed his arms away.

Jared said, "Mmm—hmm?" as he reached for her again. Damn, she was all supple warmth wrapped around exciting responses. A firecracker ready to go off in his hands. The image was still in his mind when she began to wriggle, and he whispered, "Gently, sweet; we want this to last a while. I want to last so long for you that you beg—"

Marnie got an elbow inside the crook of one of his arms and levered it sharply. With a grunt, he released her.

Though the inside of his arm throbbed with unexpected pain, he managed to ask, gritting his teeth, "Was I hurting you?"

She shook her head. Her hair swayed alluringly. Jared glared at it. The jolt from a haze of sensuality to a harshly lighted reality in which his arm hurt like blazes had been too quick to allow his sense of humor to kick in. He felt like a fool. He hurt even worse in another, more personal place than his arm, and he wasn't inclined to be amused or good-humored about it.

Then he caught a glimpse of the distress in Marnie's flushed cheeks and taut mouth. Shame swamped most of his irritability. He pushed her hair away from her face so he could see her more clearly.

"Okay, give. What happened?"

Her eyes were clouded. "I'm such an idiot."

"You feel like one, and I know I look like one. Sounds like love to me," he said with a stab at flippancy.

A flash of—something—widened her eyes for a second, then she gave him a strained smile. He hated causing her to lose her normal glow. "I'm sorry, Jared," she said miserably. "You must think I'm a tease or some kind of neurotic bitch—"

"No," he answered quickly. Marnie? She was neither. "I think something scared you. Was it me? If it was, you have to tell me what I did that pushed your panic button. Then I'll make very, very sure it doesn't happen again."

"Everything you were doing was perfect. Better than perfect. I was drowning, flying—I've never felt like that before in my life, Jared." She laid her palm shyly on his thigh. Jared told himself sternly not to react. It would be too much like masochism. Hell, it would *be* masochism, because in the last five minutes it had become pretty obvious he wasn't going to be Marnie's lover tonight. "All of it was *too* perfect," she added. "The dinner, the dancing, the boat, you . . . especially you."

Forcing himself to relax into the depths of the sofa, Jared said, "Nobody's ever considered me too perfect before." He couldn't avoid a trace of bitterness. Maybe she'd remembered his scar and belatedly discovered she couldn't hack sleeping with a man who was only cobbled together. And she didn't know the half of it. The really bad ones were still covered by his shirt.

He didn't seriously believe she'd turn away from him because he was less than perfect. But she was so fresh, so untouched. He wanted only good things for her. A long, cold drink of water on a hot day. Skies that were always blue. A lover whose body would bring admiration to her gaze, not pity. Even though she never seemed to notice the scar on his face, Jared was glad they hadn't gotten as far as unbuttoning his shirt.

Pulling up her knees, she folded her arms around her legs. "If 'nobody' realized how wonderful you are, then 'nobody' looked very closely."

"Yeah. Right."

He reached for the pack of cigarettes on the table. The first deep drag put a cloud of aromatic smoke between them.

Marnie's small, stubborn chin rested on the shelf formed by her silver-skirted knees when she doubled up her legs. "It's not your fault at all. I'm just being stupid, I guess, but I've gotten out of practice of living on the level you live on. This is the kind of life I ran away from." Her eyes refused to meet his.

"You're lying. Or at least you're not being honest about whatever it is that's really bothering you." He said it flatly. "I can tell."

"Jared."

"Listen, why don't we just forget the whole thing? It's late. I'll take you to a hotel." Stubbing out the cigarette, he stood up. His legs automatically braced themselves against the rocking of the boat.

Marnie's gaze dipped to the brief show of muscle under the thin wool of his trousers. As her big gray eyes traveled up his body, the impact of her sensuality hit him again. A kind of liquid weakness stole over him, accompanied by the returning flex and itch of arousal. He turned away, fast. The intensity of his reaction to her appalled him.

"Come on, let's go," he said roughly.

She stayed curled up on the sofa; out of the corner of his eye, he could see her shimmery outfit remain obstinately in place. "I don't want to forget the whole thing." Her voice was shaky but it carried conviction. "And I am being honest with you. I'm rattled. Partly because I'm back in an environment I don't visit very often anymore. But mostly because I'm not used to feeling this much. There are all these emotions bubbling up and ... they scare me. I don't mind taking chances. It's not that. Usually, though, I can calculate the odds of success and I understand up front what the penalties will be if I fail. With you—Jared, this is like falling into a river or going up in a rocket. When you touch me—well, I guess I need some time to adjust."

The pulsing need had subsided as she talked. It was replaced by relief and by a purely male satisfaction. She lusted for him. This young woman wanted him in the same way he wanted her. But she couldn't handle it—yet.

The simple knowledge was enough for now. He felt safe turning around again. "It's okay. Tonight can be a kind of preview. Nice, though, isn't it?" he asked. "That kind of chemistry?"

"Biology," she corrected him, smiling. "Guys never get that right."

"What guys?" he asked instantly.

Her smile turned into a grin. Curled up in her gown of moonbeams, she was a mischievous sprite. "Never you mind, Sarge. Nobody you have to worry about."

"I do worry, though." He held out a hand. She stood and joined him in scaling the steep stairs to the outer deck. "Your faith in human nature is going to get you into trouble. You'll end up hurt."

"Who'd do that?" A shiver ran through her when they stepped into the wind.

He slid an arm around her waist. "Me, maybe."

"You're being pretty patient with my case of the squirrellies . . ." She said it almost as a question. Her head fit nicely in the hollow of his shoulder.

The gangplank rolled beneath their feet, and he tightened his grip. "Being cautious is not being squirrelly. I could hardly complain about you taking your time when I've been preaching caution."

"That wouldn't stop a lot of people."

"Probably wouldn't, at that."

"Kind of neat to meet a man with a logical mind."

"Oh, gawd, you're not going to go feminist on me, are you?"

Ignoring his teasing comment, she switched topics completely. "Are there any telltale sorts of things to look out for when I go back to the woods at Frenchman's Lake?"

"Whoa, there!" He spoke sharply.

They had reached his car, and Jared fumbled for his keys. Finding them, he unlocked the passenger door first, and thrust her inside. Barely giving her time to whisk her short skirt into the interior, he slammed the door and stalked to the driver's side.

Settling himself beside her, he shot her a searching glance. "What does Frenchman's Lake have to do with—" he almost said *with us*, and abruptly changed it to "—with anything? Is that your campground? You can't be thinking of going back there by yourself!"

"Talking about being cautious reminded me of the sabotage," she told him amicably. "But we don't have to discuss it if you'd rather not."

"Discussing it doesn't bother me. However, contemplating you out there in the piney woods tangling with a bunch of terrorists—"

"First of all, they're not piney woods. While there are some evergreens, most of the trees are deciduous, which means—"

"Thanks," he interrupted, an exasperated edge to his voice . "I know what it means. They have leaves that fall off. Don't play the teacher with me, Marnie. I want you to promise me you won't go back there. Period."

She was quiet for a moment. He was aware of her soft breathing in the tense silence. "I can't make a promise I don't intend to keep."

"Woman—"

"Where are we going?" she asked hastily, leaning forward to peer out the front window. "This isn't the way to my van."

"I told you." Jared was holding on to his patience by the skin of his teeth. "I'm taking you to a hotel."

A large sign with copperplate script and discreet lighting revolved into view as the car rounded a corner.

"I'd really rather have access to my own transportation." The awkward stiffness in her manner clued him in. She was reverting to her damned independence on him. "If you wouldn't mind driving me to my van, I can get back on my own."

Back where? He had a suspicion she'd drive all night if nobody stopped her. Jared didn't intend to give her a chance to say she was returning to Indiana tonight. "No."

"Jared! Is there something about me that makes you think you can order me around?"

"Yeah." He pulled up to the valet parking station, put the car in neutral and jerked on the emergency brake. Then he bent across the levers between their bucket seats and kissed her. Hard.

The air went out of her in a startled peep. Blind, his fingers found the releases for their seat belts. He shifted so he could pull as much of Marnie against him as possible. Jared was vaguely aware of gears in the way and the discomfort of his position. Those things didn't matter. When she got her hands in his hair and pressed upward to rub her breasts against his shirtfront, he forgot everything but the moment and the woman.

Her mouth was sweet, warm, moist. As avid as his. Her tongue touched the tip of his shyly, then suddenly began a passionate exploration.

The door on Jared's side opened, letting in wind and cold. A young voice stuttered, "Oh! 'Scuse me!" A slam of the door failed to cover the parking attendant's heartfelt, *"Wow!"*

"Wow," repeated Marnie softly.

"Yeah," Jared agreed. He rubbed the back of his neck.

"Time to get myself a room." She touched his cheek, not the one with the scar but the other one. "I can take a cab to my van in the morning."

Like hell you will, honeybun, he thought, but he said only, "I'll walk you in."

She argued about that all the way into the glass sculpture-and-flower bedecked lobby. "Really, Jared," she muttered as the chic woman behind the desk consulted a computer screen, "I'm not some incompetent—"

"Bimbo," he provided helpfully.

"You'd better smile when you say that, soldier. I can take care of myself."

"This is a four-star hotel." Jared nodded at the lobby's deluxe furnishings. "That means it has security. Not great security, mind you, but as much as money can buy and have the owners still show an indecent profit. Adequate's not good enough. Women get mugged, robbed, raped in places like this, same as in the street."

The desk clerk glared. It was evident that she'd overheard. Jared didn't give a damn.

"Your key, miss," she said frigidly.

Marnie took the plastic card. "Thank you." Flicking her short skirt smooth with the panache of a society princess, she gathered up the bag with her dirty clothes and crossed to the elevators.

Recognizing the better part of valor when it was being flaunted under his nose, Jared did not dare offer to carry anything.

Punching the Up button, she continued to toss aggressive comments over her shoulder. "It so happens I teach hand-to-hand combat. My black belt in karate is in the wash, but I can assure you I've earned one. Maybe it's a cliché, however these hands are—"

"Lethal weapons?" he asked in her ear, urging her onto the elevator with a gentle push at her waist. They were the only passengers. With a wry chuckle, he took her hands and spread them over his chest. "I could have told you that."

He felt the sensual heat that abruptly flickered through her lick his own veins. She sighed.

"Is it okay if I play with fire here for a minute more? I know I'm not being very consistent. My hormones are realizing they aren't going to be spending the rest of the night with you." Before he realized what she was up to, several buttons on his shirt had been eased open and her fingers were slipping inside. "Do you like this?" she asked, finding his skin.

The smart thing to do would be to relax and let her fingertips search until they came to the raised, jagged lines of tissue. He couldn't. It had been a long day, a longer night. He'd had enough emotion and so had she.

Besides, there was that faint, paralyzing fear of being pitied. . . .

This was stupid and he knew it. If they became lovers, she'd have to see his chest eventually. *Just not tonight*, he thought. Frustration wasn't helping him think straight.

"Hey," he protested quietly. The rasp in his voice was deeper than usual. "This is a public place."

Her fingers stopped a fraction of an inch from the slick, dead skin. "That didn't bother you on the dance floor."

"I didn't know you quite as well then," he said without irony. "Besides, this is a preview, remember? If we keep on tempting each other, it'll be a little more than that."

The upward flicker of her lashes was wicked. Jared was glad to see her self-confidence back. "Oh, I bet it would be a *lot* more."

So did he. He couldn't let it happen. "You go brush your teeth and put on your jammies and sleep late in your nice single room. I'll have to put in an appearance at the office in—" he looked at his watch "—damn, in about four hours. I'll cut out early and pick you up for breakfast about nine-thirty. Think about what you'd like to do for the day. We can hit some museums or go sailing or whatever you'd enjoy."

The elevator deposited them on Marnie's floor. Her room was almost immediately opposite. Using her plastic key, she unlocked the door and held it open. Jared stayed where he was, just outside.

"I don't have any jammies. If you were wearing an undershirt, I'd ask to borrow it. But you're not." Her murmur was silky. "So I guess I'll have to sleep nude."

"You're trying to drive me insane."

"Is it working?"

"Yeah."

She laughed, but she was looking at him curiously. "You like museums? I wouldn't have pegged you for the type," she said.

"No," he admitted. "But I'd like to be with you. I thought museums would appeal to a woman who ran away to see some cave hallowed by the whoever-it-was."

"The Delphic Oracle. Two thousand years ago, it was really famous. Like Dear Abby or Ann Landers."

"Don't ever let anyone tell you Marnie Rainbrook isn't cut out to be a teacher."

She laughed self-consciously. "Okay, no more history lectures tonight. You're in luck, Sarge. I don't feel any particularly strong craving to stare at paintings or dinosaur bones tomorrow. I'm going back to Frenchman's Lake."

Damn. "Oh, no, you're not."

She tossed the department store bag into her room to free her hands. They planted themselves on her hips. His lips twitched. Her belligerent pose was spoiled by the pure sensuousness of her silk tunic, and the way her hair tumbled in Rapunzel-like profusion. "Get this, Sarge, you get it good. Take the proprietary attitude you seem to be developing and flush it down the—"

"Can you listen for a minute?" he interrupted. At least she hadn't said paternal attitude. "A booby-trapped forest is no place for an amateur."

Marnie said something crude, and went on swearing with an earthiness that reminded him she spent her time with teenage boys—although her vocabulary outstripped the normal repertoire of four-letter words. There were even a few words he'd never heard before. On the whole, Jared got her drift. He'd served his time in the army, after all, and the give-and-take in an office like his could get pretty salty. Fragile-looking, fairy-like Marnie would have fit right in.

The fact remained that there was no way he was going to let her wander off into the woods to play girl sleuth. Especially on the trail of people crazy enough to drive spikes into trees.

"All right, that's enough," he said. "You're big, you're tough, you've got a black belt in karate and you can chew your way around cusswords like a drill instructor. It's still ridiculous for you to go out there alone. To go out there at all. You saw some spikes and some wires. What about grenades? Sometimes they're attached to trip wires. Do you have the training to defuse them? Leave the whole thing to your board of directors. If they've got any sense, they'll call in the authorities."

"You—you—" Apparently Marnie had run out of names. She leaned back against the door so abruptly it slammed against the wall. Jared could feel the ache of her frustrated unhappiness in his own gut. God, he'd been so scared he would make her unhappy. And he had. "We just keep going round and round, don't we?" she asked. "Maybe it's just as well you and I aren't falling into bed together. Because if you can't treat me as an equal, then I'm not interested."

They stared at each other.

She was so young, so filled with the belief that dangers couldn't really hurt her. Jared felt every one of his forty years.

Carefully, he lied, "My hang-up is hearing the women I'm with use foul language. How I feel about that has nothing to do with my opinion of their competence. I also tend to have strong feelings about having my dates put themselves into situations where they can get blown up."

There, Jared congratulated himself. *That went pretty well.*

But Marnie straightened. "Your women. Your dates. It's okay for you to cross-examine me about my sex life, but I'm supposed to put up with being one of a herd, right?"

"That's not—"

"Don't try to talk until you get that foot out of your mouth—you might hurt yourself. Go away, Sarge. I'll do my best not to get blown up next trip to the woods."

The door closed neatly in his face.

8

THE KNOCK ON THE DOOR was light but firm. Conscious of how much skin was revealed by the short robe, compliments of the hotel management, Marnie tightened the matching belt and turned the knob.

The person outside wasn't a bellboy or maid with her laundry, as she had expected. Instead, Jared stood there.

Sunlight rushed through the windows behind her and danced off the highlights in his coppery brown hair. It was early—not quite eight. In low-slung jeans and a buttoned-up khaki vest he looked revoltingly fit for someone who hadn't left her side until after one and therefore couldn't have had much sleep. Marnie had already scrubbed her face and braided her hair, but she still felt cranky and disoriented. She'd had less than five hours sleep herself.

After the final disagreement with Jared, she had lain awake counting all the mistakes she'd made with him. First she'd been too pushy, then too cautious, then too damned hurt and insulted to talk him out of his idiotic conviction that she wasn't fit to be let out alone. She'd been taking care of herself since she was thirteen, for crying out loud. Generally she was too busy to be lonely and too self-sufficient to require a man for entertainment, but . . . sometime around four a.m., she'd faced the fact that she wanted Jared in her life. It was crazy to fall for a man so sexy, so full of animal grace— not to mention so successful—that he probably had as many chances with women as there were women who'd take chances. But that was precisely what she'd gone and done. And meeting, attracting and scaring him off all within three days would be too quick and brutal.

"You're not my dry cleaning," she said, suddenly happy.

He gave her his slow half grin. "No, ma'am," he said. "I see you didn't have to sleep in the buff last night."

Stepping back so he could enter, she decided to punish him, just a little. "Actually, I put on the robe so I wouldn't shock the bellhop."

He dropped into a chair. "Go easy on my blood pressure, honeybun. I haven't been to bed."

"Not at all? Oh, Jared." Maybe they weren't going to talk about last night's arguments. That was fine with her. Atop a small courtesy refrigerator a coffeemaker dripped life-giving liquid. Marnie poured him a cup.

"Thanks." He sipped, closing his eyes.

The unmade bed suddenly seemed too rumpled, too inviting. Marnie tidied it, making ruthless hospital corners and snapping the coverlet to smooth the middle.

"Let's get one thing straight," he said, peering at her through slit lids.

"Okay."

"I am not looking for a quick lay and I'm too old to have the energy or the time to satisfy a herd of women. Got it?"

She bit her lip. "Gotcha."

"Even if I did happen to be a satyr, which I'm not, I would've had to get rid of any harem I was keeping once I met you. Ask why."

"Why?" she repeated.

"Because if I didn't, I'd be fairly sure you'd cut off what it takes to keep a herd of women satisfied."

"That would be cutting off my—nose—to spite my . . . I don't think I can finish that thought." Her flip courage gave out halfway through the joke, and heat flooded her cheeks.

Jared's sleepy eyelids looked very sexy. "I love watching you blush. You're an innocent, know that, Marnie Rainbrook?"

"I told you last night I'm not a virgin. You don't have to protect me from the big, bad world."

"Innocence doesn't necessarily have anything to do with how many guys there have been," he said dryly. "The number of times isn't as important as how you felt about them." He studied her face with amusement. "Damn, Marnie, you are a Victorian. You talk like a '90s woman, but boarding school is about your speed. Can't you believe I don't care whether or not I'm first in line? As long as the line stops with me."

Maybe Jared didn't care. But Marnie realized she did. Compared to the glorious confusion of feelings bubbling up inside her, the emotions inspired by her previous boyfriends had barely been ripples. She'd tossed away something that would have had value if she'd given it to Jared.

A few moments ticked by while she regretted the might-have-been. If Jared could have been first . . . but there wasn't any point brooding about it. She pushed the conversation in a different direction. "If you came back here to pick a fight—"

"I didn't."

Another knock interrupted him. Marnie opened the door to a maid, who had yesterday's jeans, shirt, socks and underthings dangling from hangers inside clear plastic. Accepting them with a smile, Marnie handed the maid a tip and closed the door.

"Excuse me," she said to Jared. "I'll, uh, get dressed now." She headed for the bathroom.

His chuckle stopped her. It was a very satisfied sort of chuckle. "That's what I thought."

"Now what are you talking about?"

"You. I've finally got a fix on what makes Marnie tick. You're what I thought you were the first time I saw you."

She pushed her braid off her shoulder. "And that is?"

"A nice girl. A very, very nice girl."

"Sarge, you're full of it."

Getting up, he ambled to the coffeepot and poured himself another steaming cupful. "Full of what?" he asked, grinning in a way that told her he was remembering the abuse she'd flung at him last night.

"Delusions!"

She'd have to apologize to David, Marnie thought as she slammed the bathroom door behind her and stripped off the robe. Being called nice *was* the ultimate insult.

But when she regarded her image in the mirror, the face looking back at her was smiling.

She inspected the rest of her body. The expression in the mirror grew distant, absorbed. Slender neck, square shoulders, small breasts high and firm on a long torso; trim waist and hips, legs long enough to balance everything else, and muscles that didn't show. The curls at the apex of her thighs were the same dark blond as her French braid; it occurred to her that Jared didn't know the color was natural. She touched one wisp with a questioning finger. Would he say anything about the color if she walked out as she was this very instant?

Males were supposed to be impressed by natural blondes.

Then Marnie caught sight of her hand in her mirror image and flushed from the tops of her breasts to the roots of her hair. She snatched her hand away and grabbed her panties.

The buttons on the man-tailored plaid shirt buttoned all the way to the neck. With crisp movements, she fastened all of them. Finishing her dressing took a bare minute. Another quick glance at the mirror confirmed that she looked to be a completely different woman from the one wearing the same clothes yesterday. Of course, she didn't usually have her grubbies professionally cleaned. Today the starch in her faded black jeans gave them style. Her flannel blouse practically crackled. The predominant blue in the pattern flattered her fair skin, while the gray stripe matched her eyes and the soft yellow line echoed her hair's blondness. There wasn't anything she could do about her boots. They were just . . . boots. Not dainty whimsies of fashion, but clunky practical footwear. Visible symbols of where she was going and what she planned to do.

"I'd better be on my way," she announced, letting herself out of the bathroom.

Jared was standing by the window; he turned and said, "I don't suppose we have time for a little nap first?"

Because the sun was behind him, his face fell into shadow. The backlighting emphasized how big and tough he looked. And was.

Last night's resolutions weakened. A little nap and a lot of loving sounded preferable to a long drive and a tramp in the woods. Rubbing her hands on her thighs to expel tension, she answered, "Please, Jared, really,

I'm not ready for that yet." Her tone wasn't very convincing.

"That what?" he asked. Angling his path slightly, he walked toward her. Sun lit one side of his face—the scarred, dangerous side, she noted absently—and she could see his brows draw together. "You mean— Oh, that."

"Yes," she said, feeling goaded. "That. Sex."

His forehead cleared. "Damn, you must think I'm Superman. I hate to disillusion you, but a night on the town and an early morning spent swearing at a computer aren't the best preparation for...that. When I say sex, I mean sex. All out, all night sex. But when I say nap, I mean sleep."

"Oh." Her cheeks were so hot they flamed.

"I'm flattered, though." He came close and smiled down at her. "You're beautiful when you blush."

Marnie hadn't known she could be this flustered. She thought frantically, trying to come up with a dignified exit line. The best she could do was to say again, "I'd better be going."

He groaned and put his cup next to the coffeemaker. "I guess we should. The bag is all you're taking, right?"

"Right, but—what do you mean, *we?* I told you, I'm returning to Frenchman's Lake."

"And I heard you, lady, loud and clear. If you'll recall, I said you weren't heading back there by yourself." As Marnie blinked up at him in astonishment, he picked up the shopping bag, which now contained her pretty things from last night, and steered her toward the door. "Don't get me wrong. I'm not some goddamned mercenary. I'm just an ex-soldier with rusty skills. But I'm better than nothing. Get this, though. I'm in charge. I make the rules. When I say back away from something, you don't stop to ask me why. You just do it. Understood?"

"Understood." She sighed. "You've got a fixation about rules, Sarge."

"Maybe. I won't argue with you about that as long as you do what I tell you to do when I tell you to do it. If that's clear, let's go."

PICTURE-PERFECT countryside skimmed past, vividly green with growing things. Chicago lay behind them. Marnie decided the memories of the last twenty-four hours could be folded and wrapped and put away as neatly as the silk evening outfit in the department store bag. Right now it was enough to be driving toward Frenchman's Lake with Jared sleeping beside her.

The van bucked in the wind.

"I haven't used a form of transportation this—utilitarian—since Nam," remarked Jared, stretching himself awake.

"Snob," she replied without rancor.

"It's not being snobbish to object to your riding around in an engineering dinosaur. It's so top-heavy every gust of wind threatens to overturn it. The lighting's so bad you can't see all the way to the rear inside even with the overhead light on. And it's pink, for God's sake."

"Violet. I don't like pink."

"The license plate reads, Her Van. Haven't you ever heard of muggers and rapists targeting vehicles that look like they belong to women? Sleazes hang around parking lots waiting for the owners to show. Somebody could hide in the back and you'd never know it until he chose to pop out."

The possibility had never occurred to her. Jared's words called to mind an image of a rapist leaping into view like a jack-in-the-box. She suppressed a quick shiver. "Okay, you convinced me. I'll get a paint job and a new plate."

"How about a new car? This one's made out of aluminum foil." During another momentary lull in the otherwise steady breeze, the chassis bounced on the tires; Marnie corrected her steering, hunching her shoulders. Nobody else could stimulate her as much as Jared did—or get her to feel so defensive. Damn the man.

"I like having a van. And mine has one big advantage. It's paid for."

"It damn well ought to be, honeybun. The thing's as old as you are."

Without looking, she sensed Jared's frowning scrutiny. The question he didn't ask was the one she answered.

"I work for a living, and even at expensive schools like The Oaks, teachers aren't the ones pulling down the big salaries. I don't usually pour money around like water. Yesterday was—special."

He reached out and touched her neck under the heavy braid. She sensed his mood softening. "I thought it was special, too," he said.

"Thank you for driving the van to my hotel so early this morning," she went on after a moment. "Especially since you don't approve of the poor thing."

He wrapped his hand around her nape and left it there. "No problem."

"I'm especially glad you figured out how to fix the ignition after you hot-wired it."

"Can't be in the army without learning how to hotwire a car. An aptitude test they gave me showed I have a natural affinity for machines. That's how I got stuck in emergency ordinance disposal." He stretched again without loosening his hold. "I don't have much trouble with computers, either, which was good in the wee hours. I was able to leave a message for my partner, Ted, and instructions for the staff who'll be covering for me over the next few days. But I didn't mean to go to sleep on you."

"That's okay." She darted him a look. "You made it clear letting you rest might have some, uh, advantages."

The slightly rough ends of his fingers tickled her neck. "Does that mean you're rethinking the readiness issue?" he asked in his gravel-edged voice.

Marnie tried to concentrate on the road; it wasn't easy with his hand slipping inside the collar of her shirt. "Thinking about it, yes." As much as she could when he touched her.

Maybe thinking was overrated.

She didn't really believe that. The way Jared made her libido run riot was tied up in a grab bag of other responses. He was a hero. His action the day of the parade had been enough to make him larger than life in her eyes. Today he'd broken one of his own rules and destroyed his schedule to take her on what he regarded as a wildly quixotic venture. A hero, even if a reluctant one.

He'd said he wasn't a mercenary, and that was true. There wasn't any money in this. Nor did Jared expect to be paid with sex. That he was willing to help was simply her good fortune. That's what he was—her soldier of fortune.

The sun was a bright yellow ball, the sky a glazed, porcelain blue. Ahead, puffy clouds formed monsters only children could believe in.

"The day's too pretty for thinking," Jared said.

She let her head fall back so she could rub it against the edge of his hand. "You're right, Sarge."

9

"LUNCH?" Jared asked as they approached an exit off the interstate.

The van wasn't quite within reading distance of the sign that would indicate which hamlet they were nearing. Marnie didn't need to squint to know what it would say. She shifted uncomfortably. "It's a little early, isn't it?"

"Not if the last solid food you saw was a maple bar at six o'clock this morning," he pointed out. "Did you even eat that much for breakfast?"

"Well, no."

"Come on. As long as it won't upset your feminist principles, I'll pop for the bill. You can't turn that down. A free lunch."

She gripped the wheel. "If you want to stop, we'll stop. But there won't be any bill."

The sign loomed closer. Rainbrook: Exit ½ Mile.

He did a doubletake as the sign flashed past. Marnie slowed the van.

"I take it there's a connection, Ms. Rainbrook?" he asked.

"Great-great-granddaddy founded the town," she said in resignation. "As you can tell from the name of the place, he had quite an ego. He also had a bank. The Illinois Rainbrook Guaranty and Trust. Not big or famous, but very stuffy. Very hidebound. The Rainbrooks are into old money and strict rules."

"So that's how you could afford to run away to Greece. Must be convenient having a bank in the family," he said mildly.

She shrugged. "Depends. The experience taught me not to rely on credit. My family was able to trace me through charge card receipts."

"You stole a credit card?"

The exit crept up, and Marnie maneuvered onto the turnoff with aching slowness. Reluctance to visit home rather than safety was her motive. Impatient with herself, she put her toe to the gas pedal. The van rolled onto Main Street at precisely the speed limit. The granite facade of the Illinois Rainbrook Guaranty and Trust rose above the other buildings in the middle of town.

"You don't get it, do you?" she said, as she aimed the van down a broad, tree-lined street. "The idea was to fix it so I didn't have to steal. My father and stepmother had given me my own charge cards. I was thirteen years old, and I could draw on an unlimited amount of credit."

"That's insane."

"Yes, it is."

"And now I'm going to meet your parents." He said it with what in another man she would have described as foreboding.

"I can't very well come through town and not stop to see them. They'd hear about it and be hurt. I really don't like to go out of my way to hack at their feelings. They're disappointed enough in me as it is. I'm the maverick in the family."

Jared released his breath in a hard sigh. The situation was his own fault; Marnie had tried to avoid it gracefully, and he hadn't let her. Best to fake it. Ignore the natural male aversion to being introduced to a woman's parents. Especially when the woman was young and he intended to bed her.

But, *hell*, what if he and Mr. Rainbrook were practically the same age? It wasn't impossible.

She pulled the van to a stop in front of a huge, shady corner lot and switched off the ignition. Tall maples dotted an acre of velvety lawn. Dominating a rise in the ground was a sprawling house, half native rock, half tan clapboard. Stained glass filled many of the windows, and one whole wing jutting off to a side was walled in clear glass.

The woman who answered the double, oak doors couldn't have been less than sixty. She was a solid, grandmotherly type. Her arms enfolded Marnie in a warm hug. "Love bug!" she exclaimed, letting go only after a long minute. Tears sparkled behind her bifocals.

The stepmother whose forte was shopping? Jared didn't think so, and Marnie confirmed his guess by answering, "Ellen, it's so good to see you. I hope your arthritis is better. Here, I want you to meet my—Jared. Jared Cain, this is Ellen Hippensteel. She's the lady who put hydrogen peroxide on my scraped knees when I was a kid and, boy, did it sting. She also taught me how to bake chocolate cakes."

Housekeeper, then. A plain gold band circled the ring finger on her gnarled left hand. He said, "Hi, Mrs. Hippensteel."

A sharp gaze replaced the tears. "Your Jared, is it? And do *they* know about your Jared?"

Marnie shot him an apologetic glance, rolling her eyes. "Shout it louder, Ellen. Maybe they didn't hear you."

"No sass from you, young lady. I've still got that bottle of hydrogen peroxide around here someplace."

"Child abuse," Marnie said mournfully. But her arm went affectionately around Ellen's wide waist as they all entered a dark-panelled hall. "My knees don't happen to be scraped today. Ask Jared."

"Seen 'em this morning, has he? And you're not ashamed to tell me so."

"No, I'm not ashamed." A rueful smile played around her mouth. "However, if you don't knock off the inquisition, Jared's going to cut and run and then where will I be? A pathetic lone female, withering on the vine. . . ."

Ellen gave her a little push. "What are you talking about? Best thing ever happened to me was that bastard Hippensteel going out for a beer March 15, 1956, and never coming back. I went and got me a good job and I've kept it near forty years, arthritis or no arthritis. Depending on myself has given me a lot better life than I would have had waiting for some man to provide for me, I can tell you."

"I thought you would."

Her smile had turned mischievous less than halfway through Ellen's speech. It brightened the gloom of the hall, Jared thought, even though the joke appeared to be directed at him. Ellen's declaration of independence had the sound of a story told many times before and Marnie must have known which conversational button would get Ellen to repeat her philosophy of life. She'd pushed that button so he would hear it.

"Ellen's got you pegged," he muttered, holding her slightly back as they followed the housekeeper through an equally somber living room. The walls and furniture were opulent but dark. Cold, stale air ruffled the hair on his arms. The room gave the impression of a well-furnished cave. He wondered what it must have been like for Marnie as a child, growing up in all this tasteful gloom. Into her ear, he said, "You are sassy. Message received loud and clear."

Pushing aside a tasseled drapery, Ellen led them into a room that exploded with light and warmth in comparison to the dank chill they'd left behind. The play of color and light was so dazzling that it took a moment for Jared to focus on the two people who stood as he and Marnie entered.

"Marnie darling!" The first to move was a woman of about Jared's age. An expensively tailored skirt and blouse didn't quite tame her curvaceous figure. She crossed the room to catch Marnie's hands in her own beautifully manicured fingers and planted a kiss in the air by Marnie's cheek.

"Hello, Louisa. You're looking wonderful, as always."

Marnie retrieved her hands and went to the man still standing by a love seat. "How are you, Father?" They placed grave kisses at the corner of each other's mouths.

"Gout's bothering me again." Gazing over her shoulder, Mr. Rainbrook gave Jared a shrewd up-and-down glance. "Wouldn't believe in this day and age a man could still be afflicted by an old-fashioned thing like gout, would you? But it's true."

"Then you should be taking it easy," Marnie scolded him. "Here, let's all have a seat." They did, Mr. and Mrs. Rainbrook in their previous positions, and Marnie and Jared in camp chairs with floral cushions. Hanging plants twisted slowly in the disturbed air currents. "We've invited ourselves to lunch. Um, this is

Jared Cain. Jared, my father Arthur Rainbrook and my stepmother Louisa."

A pause followed the introductions. Jared was acutely aware of the sharp glances Marnie's parents kept shooting at him. Did everyone in this household specialize in knifelike stares?

Was how he felt about the daughter of the house so apparent?

"Is that place where you work closed for some reason, darling?" Louisa asked at last. "We never see you on a weekday."

That place. Jared stirred. He had his own doubts about Marnie's hulking schoolboys, but Louisa managed to make The Oaks sound more disreputable than a brothel. Most parents would be happy to have a formerly wayward daughter in a solid, respectable occupation like teaching. As Marnie had told him, her stepmother was the exception.

"The school's open," Marnie answered. "I'm taking a few days off to—pursue a special project. Jared's helping me."

"You're a teacher, too?" Arthur said. He sounded disapproving. His distant tone fit him, somehow; inside a natty cardigan and tailored slacks, he was tall and thin. White hair lay neatly over a pink scalp that showed through here and there; his white skin was lightly dotted with age spots. Jared found it impossible to warm to the man. Still, he relaxed a little with relief. Arthur Rainbrook was at least twenty-five or thirty years his senior. If Marnie had been searching for a substitute father figure to fall into bed with, she would have been checking out men a generation older than Jared.

"As a matter of fact, I don't teach. I'm—"

"Jared's in business for himself in the city," Marnie cut in. "He's very successful. What do you think Ellen's planning for lunch? I'm starving."

As if on cue, Ellen Hippensteel stomped through the door. A huge tray was balanced in her arms. "It's ready. You said you wanted it out here, Mrs. Rainbrook."

"I think we'll eat in the dining room," Louisa decreed.

With a shrug, the housekeeper reversed her steps. The loaded tray wobbled slightly.

"Her manner is a trifle rough but . . ." Louisa's smile was the practiced simper of a woman who doesn't want to develop wrinkles.

"But her hollandaise sauce is smooth," Marnie added. "And reliable, live-in help isn't so easy to get these days. Ellen's a treasure."

Wondering why she believed the redoubtable Ellen needed defending, Jared saw Arthur take Marnie's arm in a formal fashion, so he copied his host, standing to offer his arm to Louisa. This is like a drawing room comedy, he thought incredulously. Except there was nothing remotely funny about the picture of life-loving Marnie growing up in this joyless household.

Once the four of them were seated at a table whose massive mahogany lines would have won Queen Victoria's approval, he regretted leaving the deep, casual cushions behind in the sun room. The chair prodded his backside. It felt as if it were stuffed with the original horsehair.

"Father wants the house to keep its period atmosphere," Marnie explained. She met his gaze blandly as she shifted in a vain attempt to get comfortable.

"Yeah. I can tell." Giving up, he dug into his salad.

"Louisa got to redecorate the solarium because it wasn't part of the original structure. It was built on in the fifties. Isn't that right, Louisa?"

Her stepmother turned her carefully coiffed head. A chandelier bristling with candle-shaped bulbs cast a brassy light over her titian-tinted hair. "Yes indeed. You were going to describe exactly what it is you do, Mr. Cain. Please go on."

Someone's toe connected with his shin. Since Louisa, who sat kitty-corner to him, didn't seem to be the type to play footsie, he assumed Marnie had aimed a kick from directly across the table. It didn't take a rocket scientist to figure out what had brought the worried cloudiness to her eyes.

Conventional bankers were notorious for their prejudice against those who wheeled and dealed for a living, as he did. That didn't stop some of them from engaging in similar practices. He'd met bankers who were like gamblers in Las Vegas splurging with money that didn't belong to them. But Arthur couldn't be the kind of financial officer who put customers' funds into chancy projects the bank wasn't set up to handle. Jared had never heard of Illinois Rainbrook Guaranty and Trust . . . and he would have if it was in the governmental hot water drowning a number of other institutions.

There wasn't any point in hiding the truth about the way he made a living from Marnie's parents. He tried to grin reassuringly at her. Jared was never more aware of his one-sided smile.

"I own half of Cain and Marshall Associates. We're a commodities brokerage house."

"Commodities?" Arthur's nose thinned, as if the portion of perfectly-baked-from-scratch chicken pot pie Ellen was setting before him smelled bad.

"I think if you check us out, you'll find we have a pretty good reputation. The firm's been lucky."

"Luck!" Arthur retorted. Jared had been right about what smelled off to Marnie's father; the older man chewed a morsel of chicken vigorously and jabbed the tines of his fork at Jared. "You can't build a future on luck. No depending on it."

Despite himself, Jared couldn't keep his fingers from stroking the scar that ran down his cheek. "I'd have to agree with you there."

IF CONSERVATIVE BANKING practices had bought the Rainbrook home, Rainbrook could keep them, Jared thought. The place gave him the willies.

All the old, valuable things in it only increased his sense of claustrophobia. There were too many oppressively framed oil paintings by artists he'd actually heard of, as well as too much cut crystal but not enough light.

The only bright spot was Marnie. She had changed the subject to movies. Good manners on Arthur's part, as well as indifference on Louisa's, had kept the conversation from returning to the personal realm.

After the pot pie, Ellen entered with dessert cups teetering on a glass platter. Her mouth was tight—with the pain of arthritis, Jared thought—and her swollen fingers clutched loosely at the handles. Marnie's attention was being held by something her father was saying. Jared could see the inevitable coming and got quickly to his feet. He was an instant too slow. The cups, which were filled with lemony-looking pudding, and then the platter slid to the hardwood floor.

The crash of shattering crystal was shocking in the quiet old house.

"I don't believe this. My grandmother's Irish crystal!" Louisa fumed openly. "Oh, go get a scoop and a mop and clean this mess up." Barely waiting for the housekeeper to leave the room, she threw her spoon on the table. "This is the last straw. Last month she broke the Belleek dancing bear. I'm replacing Ellen. She can work until I find someone else."

Marnie swivelled in her chair. "Hell, that's gracious of you, Louisa. Why don't you wait for December, so you can fire her just in time for Christmas?" Her eyes sparkled with indignation. "Maybe somebody left out a lesson when you went to Lady-of-the-Manor School. You don't simply can a faithful servant after thirty-six years."

"Of course we wouldn't just let her go," Arthur struck in. "Ellen has a very reasonable retirement package. She won't be in want."

"Take away her work and she'll shrivel up and die. You'll push her into feeling old. The arthritis already makes her defensive. Besides, Ellen's lived in this house longer than I did. Longer than Louisa, if it comes to that."

There was a silence. The elder Rainbrooks looked carved from stone; Marnie looked guilty. Jared shifted on his hard chair.

"That remark was uncalled for," Arthur rebuked her.

Pushing back her chair with a scrape on the highly varnished floorboards, Marnie knelt on the floor and began to pile slivers of custard-splattered glass into a spittoon that had been parked near an old-fashioned sideboard.

"I was out of line," she agreed, not looking up. "I beg your pardon, Louisa."

Jared joined her. The crystal had shattered into shards that glittered against the dark oak. The bits of broken glass pinged as he and Marnie dropped them into the spittoon.

"I don't know anything about dancing bears," he said, "but it was my fault Ellen dropped the platter. I moved and startled her. The sentimental value of an heirloom can't be replaced. However, I'll naturally do my best to find you another just like it."

Struggling visibly, Louisa regained her composure. "Please don't bother. It was very old. I doubt a similar antique can be had at any price."

Her reply was so frosty that Jared promised himself he'd get the damned woman an identical damned platter no matter how long it took or what it cost.

Ellen came back with cleaning equipment and firmly declined Marnie or Jared's help.

"We'd better be going now," Marnie said, subdued.

Jared hated seeing her normal glow dampened. Grabbing her hand, he steered her rapidly toward the door, and freedom.

But in the hall, Louisa drew Marnie to one side and talked to her in an earnest undertone, leaving him with Arthur. Marnie's father touched the collar of his natty sweater in a nervous gesture, and said, "May I assume you're interested in Marnie?"

"Yeah, you can," Jared answered bluntly. He waited.

The response wasn't what he expected. Looking at his daughter, Arthur said, "She's a good girl, you know. Sound instincts. Louisa wanted a different life for her, but the day of debutantes is over. Teaching's not a bad career. No money in it, of course. Still, as you may have guessed, there's no lack of financial support from her family—for her or the man she eventually marries."

"She seems to be a tad independent." For sweet, suffering Pete's sake was the man courting a complete stranger for his daughter? "And I didn't get the feeling you cared much for me or what I do for a living. Why tell me this?"

Rueful pride pursed Arthur's lips. "We just want her happiness. Independent is exactly what she is. But whether she chooses to acknowledge it or not, she isn't without resources from her family. Our daughter's husband will have our backing." He looked at Jared meaningfully.

"Mr. Rainbrook, I don't know what conclusions you've reached about me, but I'm not an opportunist." He almost said not a mercenary. "If this is some kind of trap to discover if I'm a fortune hunter, it won't work, because I'm not. And if you're implying Marnie can't get a man without the added attraction of her family's money, all I can say is, you haven't taken a good look at your daughter lately."

A slow smile almost brought animation to Arthur Rainbrook's austere features. "You can't blame me for doing my best to find out what kind of man she's brought home."

The hell of it was, Jared couldn't. It was probably the sort of thing he'd do, too—if, God help him, he ever had a beautiful young daughter to protect.

When Marnie rejoined them, the slant to her mouth could only be described as mutinous.

"Bye, Father," she said briefly.

Jared added his goodbyes, and they escaped. "Want me to drive?" he asked.

"Okay."

Instead of heading back toward the interstate, he drove the pale purple van into Rainbrook's small downtown area. There was a shop he remembered from their quick drive through town . . . the sign read Steve's Antiques and Collectibles. The van fit in an empty space, after some tricky parallel parking. He blessed the quirk of fate that had left both his eyes intact in the explosion that had sliced and diced the side of his face and chest.

"Coming in?"

"I think I'll stay in the car." He could see the effort her smile cost her.

Jared gave her braid a tiny tug. "You did the best you could for Ellen, honeybun. Some situations you can't change."

"You're a fine one to talk, taking responsibility for the whole thing. Are you really going to replace the platter? It'll cost a mint. Want to go Dutch on it?" His answering expression must have been forbidding, he realized, because she glanced at him and flushed. "Or I could pay for it. That would be the way to go. I could—"

"You could sit in the car," he bit out. "I'll take care of the damned thing. You are not paying. No way. That's against the rules. This is my folly. Try to behave yourself while I'm gone."

Her smile became a fraction less strained. "Yes, Sarge," she said.

"Let's hope Steve knows his stuff," Jared muttered as he shouldered his way into the shop.

He did. Not only was the round little antique dealer knowledgeable about glassware, he'd seen the platter in question at a party given by Louisa and was able to locate a duplicate in a sellers' catalog within minutes.

"We'll take it." Scrawling his signature on a check, Jared glanced out the display window, which was crammed with expensive junk, old and new. Marnie's profile was brooding.

When he climbed back into the van, however, she flashed him the familiar easy smile. "Mission successful?"

"You got it." He switched on the ignition and revved the engine to gauge its horsepower. It coughed and then responded with an asthmatic growl.

"Ever consider a tune-up?" he asked, pulling into the sparse traffic.

"I do all that stuff myself," she said blithely, "with some help from the mechanically-minded kids at school. I've got one new student who's like you—really a whiz with machines. I told you about him last night. Kevin . . ."

They talked for a while about work and friends. Veering east, Jared crossed the state line and began the southward crawl through Indiana on highway 41. By the time flatland began to bunch up into a series of rolling hills, the conversation had declined into a comfortable silence.

Jared broke it. "What did your stepmother have to say about me? She didn't appear altogether happy."

"How do you know you were the topic under discussion?"

"Male intuition."

She burrowed into the seat. "Mmm," she said noncommittally.

"Let me put it this way, Marnie. I'm sixteen years older than you are. My face makes it fairly plain I was once in some kind of fight. A fight I lost. And I'm in a line of work I happen to like and am good at—but I can't deny it's chancy." His brows were so tightly knit that pain twinged behind them. He wasn't going to tell her the trick her father had tried to play. "Most mothers would have a problem with all of those facts. At least, that's what I'd imagine."

"Come on, Sarge," she said lightly. "You've never been a mom."

"I never had a mom. Maybe you should know the whole list of reasons why Louisa would be right for warning you off me. My mother walked away from the hospital the same day I was born. The moment she could dress herself and sneak out. There never was a father. My adoptive parents split the year I went into kindergarten. It was foster homes after that."

"Oh God, Jared."

"My education was a shambles. I used to dare teachers to get me to learn anything. Not many of 'em did. Instead of waiting for the draft, I signed up after I dropped out of high school. If we hadn't been at war, I doubt the army would have wanted me, but they were taking everybody then. Guys like me used to be called cannon fodder. In Nam, we were just grunts."

He fumbled for a cigarette.

"There wasn't much to do for entertainment when we weren't on duty except smoke dope and boff bar girls. I'd seen too much of what dope does, and I wasn't enthusiastic about catching what the bar girls were passing around from one soldier to another. So I had free time on my hands. I put it into studying for my high school equivalency exam. Then I was promoted on the field twice."

"That doesn't surprise me," Marnie said.

"It wasn't for my natural leadership abilities, honeybun. Mines have a tendency to blow up before they can be defused. What you might call opportunities at higher rank opened up frequently. Emergency ordinance disposal wasn't exactly a plum assignment. I was promoted over other men's dead bodies. Literally."

"Are you trying to scare me off? Everything you're saying makes you more impressive, dummy, not less."

He grunted a curse and reached for one of her hands, pushing it under his vest. "My scintillating career as a noncommissioned officer came to the same abrupt end as those other guys'. The only difference was, I didn't quite die. Only one of the scars stops at my chin. Another one starts at my collarbone."

He heard her gasp. Warm fingertips searched until they found the raised skin. The moment of discovery ought to have been easier while he was driving, because his survival instinct told him his attention was required on the road. But no. Tissue he had always believed to be dead still possessed life and feeling. The soft tracing of her fingers burned up his abdomen and over his chest.

She laid her palm over his heart, and he could feel it beating. "Not all of us carry our wounds on the outside. Could you pull over for a minute?"

Jared obeyed, because he was staring at the road and not seeing it. His cigarette burned unheeded in the pullout ashtray. But he ground out in a harsh voice, "Why?"

"Sarge, for a guy with the smarts to pull himself up by his own bootstraps, you ask the silliest questions. I want to kiss you, that's why."

10

THERE WAS TIME for one incredulous flash from his brown eyes, and then his mouth came down on hers. After that a velvety cocoon cut off everything but the urgency of his lips and tongue, the hard warmth of his chest—his mangled chest that felt so good crushing her breasts....

The kiss ended too soon. "How can you set me on fire in a hippie nightmare of a van parked at the side of a busy road?" he asked, his lips in her hair.

"Same way you do it to me, I suppose." *On fire*. Had his body scars come from fire? The fire and blast of an explosion? A disorienting range of emotions raged within her—compassion, excitement, desire.

The look he aimed at her was full of frustration. "Can you give me some kind of timetable on . . . forget it."

"What?"

"Never mind. I was going to be crass. You don't deserve that." Gently, he removed her eager hands from his body and set them in her lap.

"It could be that I do deserve it. I'm not normally a tease, Jared. Were you wondering if I have a timetable for going to bed with you?"

He started the van and eased it back onto the asphalt. "Something like that."

She swallowed. Her body was still humming like a top, and the sensuousness that had built up in her was so great she was aware of the muscles in her throat as they constricted and then relaxed. "No timetable. I just think it should be as soon as we have some privacy and we both decide it's a good idea." She waited a heartbeat. "Frenchman's Lake is about forty-five minutes from here."

Jared retrieved his cigarette and gave it a good, hard drag. "Is that an invitation?"

"Yes," she said steadily.

"How fast can this bucket go?"

"Sixty with a good tail wind."

He took it up to sixty-five. The college town of Bloomington flashed by. The necessity to slow as they turned onto a country road brought one of his fists pounding on his leg at the delay, and then he had to slow further when they rolled into a tiny town located at a crossroad. Behind the gas station, grocery and bar that were the main buildings, a dense forest loomed in cool, green silence.

"Do you want to stop for some supplies?" Marnie asked. "I can put together a meal from the nonperishables stored at the lake, but if you'd like bread or meat, I'll have to get it here."

Jared's sigh went straight through her. "There's nothing I want less than to stop, but I'd better pick up some, uh, stuff, too." Under his breath, he muttered, "I only hope a store this size stocks 'em."

Inside, the country store smelled equally of lemon oil and bait. Marnie hooked a plastic basket over her arm and filled it with eggs and other fresh food, while Jared wandered by himself for a few minutes. At the checkout counter, she saw that he'd found the discreetly labeled box of condoms he'd been looking for.

With a glance at her that said louder than words she'd better not try to pay, he slapped cash down on the counter for everything and ushered her back to the van.

"I guess even little country grocery stores have gotten pretty sophisticated," she commented, taking the passenger seat.

His half grin did funny things to her nerve endings. "Are you telling me the same's true of little country banker's daughters?"

Lord, was she blushing again? She hoped not. The knowledge that condoms nestled cosily next to the eggs and bread in the bag somehow made what was happening between them more real. Not like last night, when her fairy-tale bravado had dissolved into panic at how much this man could make her feel.

"Just drive, Sarge," she suggested. Her voice came out flat, because all the emotion trying to get out overwhelmed her. Jared must have sensed it; he grinned at her again and ran a warm knuckle down her cheek.

"Yes'm."

Leaving the crossroad, they drove straight into the woods. Giant trees closed over them. Within a mile, the road dwindled to a gravel throughway, and finally to a rutted track. It dead-ended in a clearing surrounded by nothing but green and brown wilderness.

"From here on, we pack in what we've brought," Marnie told him.

The supplies fit in their backpacks. The weight of the pack, plus the bedroll she'd tied on top of it, was enough to bring out a fine coating of perspiration all over Marnie by the time they reached the campsite.

Once there, she shrugged the pack off, but even wriggling her shoulders to dislodge her sticky shirt didn't help much. Turning to Jared, she was about to suggest a swim when she caught his measuring glance going over the campsite's physical characteristics.

"Lean-to in case it rains," she explained, "food locker in case we run out of bark and berries, and an out-house."

"Those I could see for myself," Jared replied. He pointed at a series of sturdy trees. "What the hell is that? Your environmental terrorists at work?"

Her eyes followed the direction of his finger, and she laughed. "The rope bridge? It's a permanent part of the installation. The kids dare each other to climb up there."

"And they're young and dumb enough to do it? Thing looks like a cat's cradle that's coming apart," he said.

Marnie reacted to his tone of tolerant amusement by catching hold of the lowest branch of a medium-size oak and swinging herself up. From the tree she grinned down at him Cheshire cat fashion. "It's perfectly safe," she insisted, lifting her arms toward the next branch. "Even if I were to fall—which I'm not—I'd land in that mess of creepers below me. Trumpet creeper and ivy. Soft as a pillow."

Firm hands grabbed her around the ankles. She could feel the bite of their grip through her leather boots.

"In a pig's eye," he said.

"Jared, what in the world—"

"In a pig's eye are you taking your tender hide up in that damned tree. Have you forgotten why we're here?"

She went very still. "I guess I have."

Viewed from above, his shoulders were as wide as planks and looked just as strong. Marnie was used to relying on herself, but this once having a pair of solid male shoulders close by was comforting. Tentatively, she patted the bark around her. No spikes, strings or wires.

"Come down," said Jared in a dangerously quiet voice. "Now."

She was happy to obey. Putting her palms on those comforting shoulders, she slid down the length of his body. He put her away from him abruptly. "I'm going to check out the rest of the camp and make sure there aren't any little surprises in the immediate vicinity."

Marnie watched him pace off the perimeter of the campsite. As she arranged the groceries in the food locker, Jared moved in a purposeful pattern over every inch of ground. He must have been a very good soldier, she thought. At last the tense angle of his shoulders relaxed and he rejoined her.

"Okay?" she asked.

"Yeah, as far as I can see without metal detectors or any other fancy equipment. I only checked the trees and bushes up to eye level, so stay earthbound, will you?"

She laughed. "Sure."

Marnie didn't look earthbound, he thought. Sunshine poured through the latticework of leaves, creating soft, dappled light. It glowed in the tendrils of honey-colored hair that had escaped her braid and lit the blue in her shirt to a jewelled tone. Her eyes were big, full of sunshine and shadows, mysterious. Fay. He couldn't quite read them. The humid air coated her skin with a layer of moisture. Her face glowed with it. All the living things in the forest—the birds, the small animals, even the trees themselves—seemed to be holding their breath.

"You want to hunt more booby traps, Sarge?"

Slowly he shook his head. "I wouldn't call what I want—"

Her fingers on the buttons of her shirt stopped him. His throat dried. Then it ached at the beauty she revealed button by button. The cloth fell to the ground in a plaid puddle. She was watching him as closely as he was watching her, and her hands strayed to her breasts and covered them.

"I wish I were more—more womanly for you."

Though he knew the eroticism of her gesture was unconscious, it brought his arousal rushing back. "You're perfect," he said. Hoarseness roughened his voice. "Marnie, so perfect."

"I thought you didn't believe in perfection."

"I do when I'm looking at it."

Her skin was smooth, a golden color above a tan line, peaches and cream elsewhere. A trickle of moisture traced a shining path into the shallow cleavage she was trying to hide. The black jeans rode her like a lover. Her body was straight, slim, athletic.

"Let me look some more," he ordered softly. He gently tugged her hands open, and her fingers intertwined with his. There was some sort of desperation in her grip that he was at a loss to account for. His glance flicked over her breasts. They were delicately made and tipped with surprisingly large, firm nipples. "You must know how exquisite you are," he said in surprise.

She bit her lower lip, making it soft and moist. "That's something hard for *me* to believe."

So the lady was slightly unsure about her desirability. Jared lost his self-consciousness about his scars in the need to tell her just how lovely he thought her. He found all kinds of things to praise about her. Soft things. Rosy things. Explicit things.

When he finished telling her, she said in a shaking voice, "I do love the way you see me, Jared."

"Good. Because I love looking," Releasing her hands, he dealt with her snap and zipper, and slid urgent palms inside the black denim. Slender hips undulated at his touch; her head fell back and the tip of her pink tongue caressed her top lip. "But I'll be doing more than just looking and touching this time, Marnie."

"Hmm." The soft sound was one of agreement. "You want a swim?"

"No, I do *not* want a swim."

Her voice still shook, but her smile was radiant with sensuality. "There's a cove just around that bend."

"I know. I saw it when I was going over the area."

"The water's like silk. It's where we all used to go skinny-dipping when we were teenagers."

"Kids' game. Practically obligatory for teenagers."

"But if you and I do it, it'll be an adult game."

Jared hesitated, and she went on, "Please. I'm all sticky. It's a gorgeous spot. And . . . I'd like to see you, too. Can't you swim?"

"Not that well," he said dryly.

Her giggle filled him with delight. "Well, gee, Sarge, what exactly do you think I'm suggesting?"

"Tell me again about how you aren't a tease." But he slipped an arm around her bare torso and walked her toward the gleaming water.

"Am I?" A shadow of worry dimmed some of her sensual glow. "One of those?"

"Yeah." They came to the water's edge. With the flat of his hand, he stroked one pouting nipple and watched it contract into a tight bud. "I like it, the way you tease me. You do, too, don't you?"

She began to work at loosening his pants. Her tongue moistened her lips again. "I—you—I feel free around you. Safe to be a little wild. Sexy. I guess teasing you's part of that. Do you mind?"

"I said I didn't, honeybun." The light brush of her fingertips around his waistband, and then up the center of his chest as she unbuttoned his vest, did nothing to decrease the urgency of his arousal. He figured the lake water would help him keep control.

Until both of them were dying for him to lose it.

Smoothing his vest back, she studied his chest gravely before resting her palms on it. The right side was okay; regulation pecs covered by a brown pelt. His short, curly chest hair simply stopped in the middle like a photograph cut in half. In his case, the other half of the picture was white scar tissue. All of his left side had been torn apart by the blast.

"It's not very pretty," he said gently.

"You know what I wanted to say to you the other day? When we met? *I'm so glad you made it through the war so I could meet you.*" She pressed a kiss onto the scars. "I can feel your heartbeat."

Drawing in a breath, Jared pulled off his jeans and briefs, keeping his eyes on Marnie as she did the same. She wasn't coy about it, and she certainly wasn't teasing now. Instead, her movements were simple and graceful and had the same unconscious sensuality that had devastated him already. A tiny breeze blew up out of nowhere, stirring the leaves on the shrubs behind her just enough to make them whisper, and clearing the air of any insects that might have designs on her luscious skin. Jared had his own designs.

"You sure you're a water sprite," he asked, "and not a wood sprite?"

Laughing, she trailed her fingers softly over his arousal on her way into the water. He throbbed, and stepped quickly after her. The cool caress of the lake helped, but not as much as he'd expected.

Marnie was already breast-high in the clear, lapping water, and as he immersed himself she drifted out another couple of feet and began to tread water. Only her head and demure hint of shoulders and arms floated above the surface of the lake. Her braid was darkened by the water to a color like brown sugar. It bobbed next to her. "This feels wonderful, doesn't it? I wanted to be all clean and wet for you," she confided.

He launched himself into an easy sidestroke. "And are you?"

"What?"

"All clean and wet?"

Reaching her, he put his mouth just below the surface of the water and fastened it to her nipple. Her gasp mingled with the *shush-shush* of the lake. He didn't try to hold her with anything but his slow, strong suckling. When the bicycling motion of her legs faltered, he put his hands under her arms to hold her up and lifted his head.

"What's the matter. Aren't you a phys ed teacher? Forgotten how to swim?"

The water had matted her lashes into black spikes. He hoped he was responsible for her dazed look. Perhaps she hadn't even heard him. "Don't stop," she whispered.

Her hands urged his head down to her other breast. In the satiny water, the nipple was cool against his lips, then it was hot and pliant in his mouth. He rolled it with his tongue and grazed it with his teeth. Her heart pounded so intimately close to his face he could feel his own pulse take on the same frantic rhythm.

He took a deep breath and plunged farther down. Halting the languid movements of her legs with a firm grip, he found the thatch of hair curling wetly over her secret flesh and slid his tongue inside.

She went completely still and rapt. Jared's air ran out before his fascination with her response did. With a scissor kick, he drove himself to the top and dragged in lungfuls of heavy Midwestern air until black spots stopped dancing between his eyes and Marnie's face.

"Had enough?" he asked, panting.

"No." Her bald answer pleased him immensely. "Oh, you mean this, uh, amphibious fooling around? It's got its points, but I think we're both going to drown."

"I wanted to give you a fantasy."

"Oh, Jared. It's a lovely one. But maybe we should pursue this on dry land."

Splashing toward the beach, Jared didn't let Marnie get far away from him. He kept his arm around her, with one hand lightly kneading a breast. She didn't seem to mind. Her body pressed itself trustingly against the side of his. Water lapped their waists, then their feet; then they left it behind and stepped onto the soft sand.

He knelt next to his jeans and from the pocket tugged the foil-wrapped circle he'd had the foresight to bring. He knew his smile was crooked. "Protection. Not too sexy, huh?"

She lay in the sand next to him, bare and natural. Fantasy? Marnie was every fantasy he'd ever had. "Everything you do is sexy," she murmured. "Does using those things turn you off?"

His glance downward was eloquent. "Do I look turned off?"

"Well, no," she admitted. "But once a guy I was with complained wearing one was like taking a shower in a raincoat. . . ." Her voice trailed off, as if she remembered Jared had a territorial streak, and didn't like hearing about other men.

Reassuring her was more important than worrying about a past she was done with anyway. "Honeybun, anybody who'd nitpick about that when he was with you wasn't worth whatever you gave him. And it's certainly not worth wasting our afternoon discussing the issue. We're both going to be protected. Period."

Still kneeling, he leaned over her and ran a thumb up the inside of her thigh. She jumped very slightly and her head fell back. Running an openmouthed kiss along the line of her throat, he said, "The sand is warm."

"Yes."

"So are you."

She touched him intimately. "You, too. Isn't it time to, um . . ."

"In a minute. I got the feeling out there in the lake we weren't quite finished with what we were doing."

The path his lips took over her body was a long one. When he got to the slight hollow below her waist, he bent her knees and lifted them over his shoulders. Her abdominal muscles tensed. He nuzzled them until she went lax again. Her legs were already open to him, and he moved lower.

"Stay as still as you can, honeybun."

Her soft, helpless moan drove him to thrust his tongue deep. Hard. Furiously.

"Oh, babe." She'd never called him a love word before, and he relished it. "Oh, babe."

The cradle his palms made under her hips enabled him to feel the fierce, tiny thrusts she couldn't hold back. When he was sure he'd given her all the satisfaction he could, he rolled away, applying the protection swiftly. Turning, he met her eyes.

They were the gray of a misty day. "Jared, I meant that to wait until you were inside me."

"Then let's see if we can make it happen for you again."

The air settled over them, almost as liquid as the lake. He played with her breasts as he filled her, taking his time. Her soft flesh closed over him, very hot, very tight. Thanks to the lake water and the humidity and the warm, earthy scents of the forest, both of them were oily with a woodsy perfume. Resting his weight on his elbows, he drew careful circles around her nipples with his thumbs.

She swallowed. "I take it you're showing me you can be a tease, too?"

"Me? Aren't I doing what you want me to do? If there's something I'm leaving out—"

Her strangled laugh ended in a gasp as he withdrew and then pushed forward again. She began to move to his rhythm.

Time was nonexistent. Marnie opened her eyes once, and saw the large, flat leaves of a sycamore nodding far above. Closer was Jared's face, dark and intent. The hair on one side of his chest and the slick, thick ridges on the other tantalized breasts that were still tender from the loving of his mouth. Their bodies were liquid.

Jared was above, she was below in a nest of fine sand. Her arms, her legs, wrapped around him and pulled his weight closer, his hardness deeper. His mouth clung to hers, demanding.

She didn't expect she would experience another explosion of sensation. Pleased astonishment still bubbled lazily within her at the shattering release Jared had already wrung from her body. She was sure it wasn't possible to reach that kind of height again so soon.

Just as she was deciding muzzily that she'd pretend so Jared would let go and take his own satisfaction, a ripple of climax gripped her. It built and reached a plateau of gentle pleasure that went on and on, and impossibly on. . . .

"Now," said Jared hoarsely, straining. "Marnie, *now.*"

He thrust deep and writhed, his whole body hard and hot. His arms clenched under her. Too tight to let her breathe, too close to let her think. Her sensations peaked, and she sobbed aloud. The spasms that shuddered through him shook her, too.

11

"I DON'T SUPPOSE you were trying to prove something awhile ago, were you?"

Jared didn't answer. He smoothed insect repellent over Marnie's back. A second splashing in the lake had washed them clean and they'd both put their jeans back on, but at his request Marnie hadn't gone looking for her shirt, discarded at the campsite. His vest was casually open. He couldn't believe he'd ever worried she would react negatively to his scars.

They were sitting cross-legged; she turned around and he calmly continued to lavish repellent over her front. "In case you *were* trying to prove something," she said, a little breathlessly, "you can rest assured that you did." The train of her thought seemed to become derailed. "Assuming you meant to. Prove anything."

Jared ran a fragrant hand down her thigh and patted it to show he was done. Taking the bottle, Marnie shoved the top of his vest aside and began spreading the stuff over his shoulders. The long twilight hours were drawing out mosquitoes.

Jared bent his head to allow her access to his neck and enjoyed the gentle stroking of her hands. His purpose while they were making love had been to put any lingering memories of her failed friend-and-lover relationships out of her mind. Permanently. His only fear had been that in his excitement, all the lessons he'd learned in the years since puberty would be forgotten—lessons about harnessing his own urgency until his partner was satisfied. There'd also been the slight fear of going crazy out of frustration. Looking at the down-tilted top of her head, he murmured, "I wanted to make it good for you. That's all."

In the dusk, her blush was rose velvet. "Are you going to turn out to be insatiable? I—I don't know if my stamina will match yours. Although you did get me to—that is, toward the end there I, uh, I did . . ."

"You did, huh? Again?" His grin threatened to split his face.

She slapped repellent on his stomach with slightly more force than necessary. "Yes, I did."

"I'm glad." Lifting her chin, he kissed her lips. Their mouths were the only inches of exposed skin not covered with repellent. "And we're very well matched as far as the sex is concerned. You'll see."

"I've already seen. And felt. But don't think you'll get away with doing all the work next time."

"Work?"

"Stop laughing. You know what I mean."

"No. Tell me."

"I'm not talking dirty when dinner has to be fixed. Unless you'd like to handle that chore, too."

"I'll help. I know how to peel potatoes. My first year in the army included a lot of KP."

"Thanks a heap, Sarge." Uncoiling to her feet, Marnie tried to glare at him and failed. Her smile spoiled the effect.

He enjoyed the novel view of her pert breasts from below. Her eyes followed the direction of his gaze and, to his delight, rather than covering herself she planted her legs aggressively apart and parked her fists on her hips.

"It so happens I know you also know that we didn't bring any potatoes."

"Okay," he said amiably, pulling on his socks and boots. "I'll burn some hot dogs for you instead."

Despite what he'd said, he was a competent cook—bachelors had to be. He knew he surprised Marnie by putting together a better than average salad and not burning the German sausages she had picked out at the grocery store. Cleaning up took time; she showed him the camp routine of washing everything washable, burning or burying the few wrappers that couldn't be salvaged and storing leftovers with scrupulous care.

"No bears around here, but there are plenty of raccoons who'll tear up a campsite if they smell food," she explained. "Even possums can be a nuisance."

He took a last puff of his before-bed cigarette and looked at the butt without enthusiasm. "I'd better bury this, too."

"If we were farther out in the woods you'd have to, but here you can just pitch it down the hole in the outhouse."

"Thank God for civilization."

The last vestiges of daylight were fading. The air was still warm, still dense and silky. He went to the outhouse and then walked the quiet trail back from the homely little structure to find that she'd zipped their sleeping bags together and set the resulting double sleeping bag inside the lean-to. Her slender form was already curled up inside.

"Would you turn off the electric lantern?" she asked.

Darkness rushed in to fill the vacuum after he shut off the lantern. As he crawled in beside Marnie, his vision readjusted to the not-quite blackness. A few feet away moonbeams dusted through the canopy of leaves.

Right in front of his eyes a tiny flashlight switched on and off. On and off.

"Fireflies," Marnie said softly. "Are you sleepy?"

"That depends. What did you have in mind?"

Her leg slid between his legs, and he realized she was naked—and warm and willing. "Showing you I'm not afraid to do my share of the work."

JARED PUT DOWN his stout stick and spritzed a careful circle in yellow spray paint.

"Another one?" Marnie looked unhappy.

"Yeah. That makes—"

"Twenty-four spikes." She swore. "How many more can there be? Forget I asked that. Stupid question."

He finished marking the location of a huge aluminum nail that had been driven into the white trunk of a big sycamore. Like all the rest of the spikes they'd found, this one was slightly below eye level. Both of them had searched higher, but they hadn't found any above five feet.

"Ready for a break, honeybun?"

"Okay. It's after eleven, anyway. Let's see what the lake has for us in the way of lunch."

Returning to the campground, Marnie slipped into the lean-to and emerged from it with a fishing pole. "I'll catch if you'll clean," she said.

"It's a deal."

Within a short amount of time, two plump catfish were sizzling in a pan over an open fire. The food locker produced imported mustard and a jar of mayonnaise, as well as leftover salad.

"I thought we were going natural," Jared remarked.

His comment won a smile from her. "What's more natural than fish you catch yourself? But I can forage for you if you like. The elderberries aren't ripe yet, but . . ." Marnie glanced around, and then plucked a frilly green twig from a plant that grew low to the ground. She held it to his lips. "Here, taste this."

He sniffed suspiciously before nibbling. "Peppermint?"

"Uh-huh. Good for tea and upset tummies. See that little bush over there? It looks about the same, but it's catnip."

Loading their plates, he said wryly, "I'll take the catfish instead." He cut a large chunk from his fish and popped it into his mouth.

They chewed in amicable silence. It was humid again, and already hot. Tropically hot. Was this what the jungle had felt like to Jared almost twenty years ago? Marnie wondered. The heat was stunning the forest's normal inhabitants into unnatural stillness; not even a chipmunk or a jay came out to scold the human invaders.

"Have you noticed anything weird about the location of the spikes?" asked Marnie.

Jared detached fish from bone. "They're all low."

"And the trees chosen to be spiked aren't the ones you'd expect. I mean, none of them has much commercial value. Environmental terrorists usually target the lumber most in demand. There are black walnuts and hardwood maples in here worth plenty to a cabinet maker. Not touched. But the sycamores aren't even good for firewood—the fumes they give off cause an allergic reaction—itching and red eyes." She wrinkled her nose. "I suppose those old apple trees would bring in a little something for firewood, but not much. The poor things are too small. Maybe they have some historical significance."

He glanced at one of the thin, gnarled brown trunks she was pointing to with her fork. "They do look historical," he agreed politely. In fact, the trees appeared to be ancient. They had wizened, brittle branches and sparse leaves.

"Well, there's a reasonable chance they were planted by Johnny Appleseed. He operated in Indiana."

"I thought he was just a legend."

"No, sir. Johnny was genuine all right—a genuine crackpot. Around here they claim smart parents used to lock up their daughters when he wandered through. Some people insist they're descended from him. He never married," she added significantly.

Jared's interest in local folklore was minimal, but he was pleased that an animated tone had returned to Marnie's voice. However, he winced slightly. "Liked 'em young, did he?"

Marnie's slow smile was mischievous with understanding. "There's no comparison, Sarge. You're not sixty, and I'm not just busting into my teens."

"*That* young?"

"That's what they say. Probably lying through their teeth. It's human nature to speculate about other people's sex lives. Not very admirable, just normal." She looked at him through her lashes. "It doesn't bother me if your friend Ted looks at us together and calls me a 'young babe.' We both know age isn't an issue between us. I think he meant it as a compliment to you, anyway."

"You have too much insight into the way men think," Jared said gravely.

"I teach fifteen-year-old boys. In a lot of ways, men stay teenagers forever. In others, grown men are definitely preferable. Remember what you said yesterday about us being, well, sexually compatible?"

"I'm not likely to forget," he told her.

Scooting across the ground, she took his arm and placed it around her waist. "I just wanted you to know, you seem to be right. We're emotionally compatible, too. Not identical, but we complement each other. You're rough and tough and persist in taking care of me whether I need it or not. I'm—oh, all right, I'm little Suzie Sunshine on the surface, and tougher than you think inside. Is it crazy to love you after less than a week?"

He used the hand not hugging her waist to fish a cigarette out of his breast pocket. "Very crazy." His lighter trembled a little as he lit up. "Hell, we're both insane."

Sitting back on her haunches, she pinned him with one of her wide-eyed stares. "Is that a declaration, sir?"

Jared had the feeling she meant her question to be teasing. But it wasn't. There was a softness, a hopefulness in her gaze, in the catch in her voice. It tore at him.

"Yes, damn your sweet eyes."

Marnie had needed some time to be ready for sexual intimacy? Well, he needed breathing space before he talked about commitment. Jared was beginning to suspect he might be capable of long-term loving. This feeling that was growing inside him for Marnie—could it erase the cynicism of a lifetime? His existence was confined to hard work and hard play, with an occasional foray into recreational sex. For God's sake, he was forty years old. It was a hell of an age to fall in love for the first time. And his code didn't allow for making deals he wasn't sure he could live with. The stakes in this gamble were too high. Marnie's happiness.

Firmly, he changed the subject. "So we've got an unusual eco-terrorist at work here?"

"I'd say so." Suddenly Marnie wasn't hungry anymore. Still, relief at Jared's refusal to say more about their relationship eased a tension in her throat. She'd brought up the topic, but as soon as the words were out in the open—*to love you*—they scared her to death. Lord, all this was happening so fast. Too fast.

They tidied up after lunch without looking at each other, and then Jared suggested, "Why don't you nap for a while? You look done in."

"I'm not a fragile flower, Sarge. We need to check for more spikes. And there are a lot of side trails where wires might be placed."

"I'm sure there are. They'll still be there after you have a rest."

Nettled, Marnie struck back. "Listen, if you're all tired and worn out, *you* take a nap. I'll go by myself."

He dropped the pan he'd been scouring with sand and started a steady, purposeful walk toward her. "No, you won't. When will you get it through your head that it's dangerous? Just because we haven't stumbled across something that could maim or kill the casual passerby doesn't mean nothing like that is out there. Be sensible. If you know how."

"Chances are okay for you to take but I'm not sensible? You are such an old—" She searched for an appropriate word.

"I'm not old," he snapped, reaching her. Clamping big fists around her wrists, he dragged her against his chest and kissed her.

"I keep telling you that!" Marnie didn't know where her anger was coming from, but it felt wonderful. Liberating. She kissed him back, so intensely she felt the imprint of his teeth, then she hooked a foot around his ankle. A tug sent them both to the ground.

They rolled and Marnie ended up on top. "The bigger they come, the harder they fall," she taunted him.

His eyes lit. "You aren't seriously challenging me to a fight?" His thick brows lowered fiercely—but his mouth twitched in a grin.

"You bet I am. I have a black belt—"

"So I heard. But you know, honeybun, it's always a good idea to find out if the guy whose eye you're spitting in has one, too." He let the information sink in. "Of course, I haven't practiced in years."

Looking limpidly into his bronze-brown eyes, Marnie brought her trapped hands sharply together and yanked down to loosen his thumbs. The idea was to attack the weakest point of his grip. It didn't work. His thumbs obediently opened, but at the same moment Jared clamped his legs over her calves and held her locked to his body. She tried using her knees on the insides of his thighs. Though his answering grunt was one of pain, he didn't yield.

"No fair," she complained. "What degree are you?" Black was the highest belt that could be earned but within that level of achievement were ten rankings of expertise.

"Sho Dan. Lowest degree. No big deal."

"Me, too. Except I worked like blazes to get it. I needed at least the Sho Dan to be an instructor. Let me up and we'll try again."

He shook his head but allowed her to rise. "I'll take you every time."

"We'll see about that."

He did, though. Once they'd removed their boots and Jared slipped off the backpack containing the spray paint, she managed to place only a few solid hits before he went on the offensive.

After that, no matter what move she made, he countered it with a movement that was faster and cleaner. His arms slashed like swords, blocking and pushing forward. The twisting kicks of his legs were so precise they were like illustrations out of a martial arts manual, and so swift Marnie felt as if she were continually stumbling over his feet as well as her own. He sent her tumbling time after time. At last he simply lay on her with a forearm hard against her throat.

"You're pretty good," he complimented her.

"Under the circumstances, I can only take that as sarcasm." She wriggled. "Okay, okay, I give up."

Lifting his arm, he stroked her hair. "No sarcasm. I mean it. You know the moves. Nice, textbook karate. I'm even willing to say I'd back you against the average mugger."

"So how come you took me five out of five falls?" she asked curiously.

"Simple. You play to play. I play to win. I used my martial arts training in combat. That gives me an edge." Levering himself up, he sat cross-legged and gave her a hand.

Marnie sprang up with lithe grace but instead of sitting or standing, she straddled his lap. Her hands crept around his neck. The anger was long gone. Exhilaration filled her.

"I can't imagine why, Sarge, but rolling around on the ground with you seems to have left me with all this excess energy. So why don't we play something we can both win?"

12

"NOW I AM WORN OUT," Jared said with sleepy satisfaction. His repletion went so deep, he didn't even crave a cigarette.

A gray squirrel, fooled by their after-love stillness into creeping close, was startled by his voice and leaped onto a tree trunk. It clung with all four small, sharp-taloned paws. Disturbed birds burst into flight; others trilled, and still others cawed raucously.

Dappled sunlight ran up Marnie's leg as she stretched it into the air. She was lying cuddled up to Jared, with the back of her head burrowed into the hollow of his shoulder. He hadn't managed to rid himself of his clothes during the frantic lovemaking—hell, he couldn't even remember at what point the two of them had tumbled down—but Marnie was beautifully bare. She pointed her toes, creating a delicate arch.

"Ballet classes?" he hazarded.

"Years of them. Until I went to The Oaks. Then—"

"Then karate." Idly, he asked, "Which did you like better?"

"What you've taught me." As if the admission made her suddenly shy, she jackknifed up, tugged her shirt from under his back and shoved her arms into the sleeves.

Was it only the shyness of a woman who was just learning the potential of her own body? His sated enjoyment fled. Getting to his feet, he straightened his own clothes slowly, watching her. "Regrets, honey-bun?"

"Oh, Jared—"

"Because if there are, we can call this off any time." He heard the tight note in his own voice. Trying to lighten it, he added, "No hard feelings."

"Well, there'd be lots of hard feelings on my part! For heaven's sake, we just made love. We *shared*. It was *important*. What's your problem, Sarge?"

Her narrow-eyed study of his face got to him; he turned his head slightly so only the unscarred side would show. God, he was falling for this girl and it was making him into a coward. Ashamed, Jared took her hand and held the warm fingers to the line that sliced through his cheek.

"You can't see the differences, can you?"

"I've already said I do," she protested. "But they don't matter. What I'm really, really tired of is having to justify us over and over again. We both have to believe we have a chance together. Otherwise it just won't happen. Think about it."

"If you're so ready to commit, why do you keep withdrawing?" he shot back. "Every time. Every damned time, Marnie."

Expressions flickered across her face. Simple surprise, then awareness as his words sank in, then a flash of resentment that quickly died. After almost a full minute of strained silence, her eyes lifted to his with painful honesty.

"I guess I do withdraw. There's so much of you, Jared—not only physically, and you're an imposing man. Your personality is forceful, too. And—and I feel you so much. I'm hypersensitive to you. It scares me that my mind has surrendered to my hormones. That's never happened to me except with you. So I back off and regroup emotionally. But I didn't know I was hurting you."

"That makes us even. I didn't know I wasn't giving you enough space," he replied carefully.

Mentally, he cursed himself. They'd known each other only a few short days. His timing was impeccable when deciding when to move on wheat futures, but Marnie meant more to him than a business deal ever could, and he kept crowding her. Unintentionally, but cruelly. The blush painting her cheeks looked hot enough to scald.

"In case it escaped your attention," she said, her chin going up, "I seduced you the last two times."

"So you did. Very well, too." Casting about in his mind for a distraction to give her the breather she needed, he remembered why they were at Frenchman's Lake in the first place. "Since you refused to take a nap, you want some more exercise instead? We haven't checked the area over there yet." He pointed west.

"That's a good idea." Her gaze slid away from his. "It's getting to be time to finish up. Both of us need to get back to our jobs. We can't spend all summer out here."

Over there was the sweep of forested ground on the outer perimeter of the property. Without making a production out of it, Marnie finished dressing, then separated from Jared to speed up the search. She had no trouble copying his system for spotting booby traps, because it was similar to the games she led at school. The basic technique was simply to watch for unusual features in the landscape. A bump on a tree trunk that sparkled with reflected sunlight, a shining strand of cobweb several horizontal inches above the earth where few spiders would weave one. Something unnatural in a green and natural world.

The work was hypnotic. Noises faded. Everything outside her direct field of vision receded into a misty backdrop. Jared moved somewhere close by; she did her best to block him out of her consciousness. Not that ignoring him was easy. He would pop back into her mind at sudden intervals . . . when she caught a hazy glimpse of his khaki vest through the trees and brush, or when an unwary movement caused muscles tender from lovemaking to give a sweet twinge. Or even when something beautiful, like a wildflower or the pattern of mottled bark on a beech, presented itself to be noticed. Her heightened awareness of lovely things served as a potent reminder that she was in love.

In love, she thought. *In love. At first sight.*

"Talk about chemistry," she muttered.

"You say something?"

"Nope. Nothing at all."

A five-petaled rose stopped her with its delicate scent. She almost tripped over a piece of plastic pipe pushing through the emerald leaves of a Virginia creeper that trailed across the forest floor. As startled by the pipe as she would have been at the sudden appearance of a copperhead with fangs ready to strike, she stumbled backward. Straight into the wild rosebush.

"Ow! Jared!"

A crash answered her. From the sound, he was carving a path straight to her through the underbrush. "Where are you? Keep talking!"

"Here," she wailed, trying to detach a branch of the rosebush from one arm. "Oh, damn, these thorns are like needles. They're embedded in my clothes and I can't get loose. No other living thing protects itself like a wild rose."

Jared reached her. He surveyed the damage. "Tell me about it," he said dryly.

"What's that mean?"

"Forget it."

The hint that Jared thought of her as a wild rose pleased her immensely. Unfortunately, at the moment, the real thing was causing her real pain. "My hair's caught, too," she said with unaccustomed meekness. "And you might want to watch out for that piece of half-inch pipe about three feet to your left."

His mouth went grim as he crouched onto his haunches, staring at the pipe from several different angles. Marnie noticed he got no closer than he had to. At last he shrugged and stood to go to Marnie's rescue.

"It'll keep. Hell, you really are stuck, aren't you?" Prying the whiplike canes from her shirt and the rear of her jeans took several long minutes.

"Now what?" asked Marnie when she was free, rubbing her bottom.

He patted her there, too, but rather absentmindedly. Marnie didn't mind, since his gaze was on the black plastic pipe.

"There are a couple of choices. I—"

"We," she said firmly.

"The pipe may or may not be connected to something that may—or again may not—explode on contact. *I* can leave the apparatus that might be buried along with the pipe strictly alone—mark the site and get the hell out of here . . . leave it to professionals with protective equipment. Or I can dig it out. If anything suspicious is attached, I can try to get it unattached. Or just haul the damned thing to the lake and throw it in."

"If it's a grenade or something, that might be hard on the fish," Marnie observed. She inched closer to him. This was another time when a large, competent male was useful to have around.

"True. But at this moment, I'm willing to sacrifice some pond life to the preservation of the greater good. You and me." He glanced at her sideways. "Honeybun, the smartest option is letting the pipe alone."

"But what if somebody else comes through? Even if we clear the leaves and twigs from around it and paint the ground, a rain squall could wash the markings away. Or the marks might be missed and then—"

"Who's the somebody that would be out here?"

"People do trespass, you know. They don't deserve to die for it," Marnie said unhappily.

"There are a couple of big assumptions behind what you're saying. We don't have any hard evidence there's a bomb buried under that pipe. Why should we expect anybody to come roaming around private property? And—" he looked into her face, and then blew his breath out through his lips "—you'd never forgive yourself if anyone got hurt, would you?" he asked resignedly.

"Probably not," she admitted. "That doesn't mean I'm crazy about the idea of you doing this particular bit of dirty work." For once she was aware of his scar, he could tell; her big gray eyes rested on it in a caress he could almost feel.

"Me, neither," he said in ready agreement. "Tell you what. Let's see what happens when we throw a rock."

He pulled her back to the maximum distance that allowed him a clear trajectory through the trees. It took some time to find a piece of sandstone that was "heavy enough to trigger a detonator but light enough to throw," Jared said, hoisting a baseball-size chunk. His pitch was straight, with a slight curve at the end. It brought the rock down within a yard of the pipe.

"Nice hook," Marnie complimented him.

"Thanks. Just to show I'm really not a male chauvinist, you want to give it a try?"

The rocks Marnie lobbed fell even closer. Then Jared dropped one barely half an inch from the pipe, but nothing resulted.

"Show-off," she said.

He grinned. "Racquetball," he explained.

They walked to their original positions. Jays were flying low in case the rocks being thrown were something to eat. At the humans' approach the birds jeered in their harsh voices and shot up into the air again. Marnie frowned at the pipe in frustration. If there was an explosive device attached to the black plastic, it remained stubbornly unexploded.

"Maybe we need to hit the pipe itself to set it off," suggested Marnie dubiously.

"Maybe." He nodded. "But we aren't going to find out. It's apparent neither of us is going to strike something that small from a safe distance—and I'm not letting you try from an *un*safe distance. Where's the spray paint?"

"You've got it in the backpack," she reminded him. She sighed, then managed a bright smile. "I'll build a cairn of rocks as an extra marker. We've certainly got plenty of them now."

One of the jays was either braver or stupider than the rest. It dove in close to investigate the strange activities of the humans. Marnie didn't think the fumes from the paint would be very good for it. "Shoo, bird," she said. "Get a life."

Her smile faded as she fashioned an arrow out of rocks, which Jared painted with sweeps of the can. She couldn't come up with a better solution for the problem . . . but she didn't like this course of action, either. The idea occurred to her that she could stay and guard the pipe—the pipe bomb?—until Jared could return with professional help. Marnie gave him a thoughtful glance and didn't even bother to make the offer. He wouldn't let her stay by herself, and she knew it. Nor was she willing to leave him here alone with his memories of a bomb that *had* gone off.

They both stepped back to inspect the pipe, now circled in gaudy yellow, and pointed to by a bright yellow arrow. The humidity was so thick that dust-mote-size droplets of paint still hung in a haze that only gradually settled to the ground.

"That's it, honeybun." Jared slung the pack over his shoulders. "Time to—"

With a snap of its wings, the jay landed on the pipe.

Jared's curse went unfinished as something went *pop* and smothering green liquid gushed up and out, covering them both.

Clawing blindly through the air until she found Jared's vest, Marnie grabbed and held on, despite the fact that it was wet with a slimy coating. Hard-muscled arms went around her fiercely.

"What the hell was that?" His voice was a deep, furious growl.

Gusts of laughter shook her. "A paint-ball land mine. I never use them at school, but I've seen them. Serious paint-ball players, adults who go in for war games, fiddle around with them all the time. They aren't hard to make for anyone who's in the least mechanical. All you need are a shoebox, a piece of piping and a spring mechanism. And the right kind of paint, of course," she added, clearing green stuff out of her eyes with a flick of her index finger.

"Don't rub that in," he said sharply. "You could be permanently blinded."

"It's harmless. Made out of cellulose—you know, vegetable matter. We'll start to smell pretty ripe if we don't clean it off soon, but that's all." Giddy with relief, she looked into his grim, drawn face and made a discovery. Her pleasure melted away. Jared's scar stood out whitely on his face. Years before he'd lived through an explosion that wasn't a joke. In spite of its ludicrous nature, this one wasn't funny at all. "You're upset."

"*Upset?* We don't call what I am *upset*, honeybun. We call it mad as hell. What kind of moron would pull a stunt like this?"

"Uh . . ." That was a good question. Marnie took a good look at the almost fluorescent shade of green and felt herself pale under her layer of paint.

"That bird doesn't think it's funny, either," he went on sourly.

The jay was hopping around disconsolately. It was so besplattered it was unable to lift off.

"Oh, Lord. Poor thing," said Marnie. "We have to rinse it off or it'll die. Other birds will attack it. It needs to be able to fly."

The backpack produced a canteen, and Jared caught the nearly immobilized animal. The moment his hands folded over it, the jay found the strength to struggle, but he held it gently to the ground despite its biting beak and frantically waving claws—and in spite of his own anger, which Marnie recognized as reaction to the strain of the afternoon.

"You're a fantastic guy, you know that?" She poured water carefully over the bird's back and wings. Ruffled blue-gray feathers began to show through as the wet paint washed away.

"Yeah, I'm a sweetheart. Watch out. I'm letting the little bugger go."

He raised his hands above his head. His arms opened wide. Startled by freedom, the jay wobbled in the air, shaking its wings. Then it shot skyward with a defiant scream and was gone.

"We'd better get cleaned up, too, " Jared said. "Damn, I'd like five minutes with the jackass who planted the spikes and the bomb."

Marnie shivered. She had no doubt that Jared was serious. He was very capable of exacting revenge on the person who'd committed these crimes.

Neither of them had been injured. Her spirits should have been lifting like the jay—straight into the stratosphere. Instead she accompanied him quietly along the trail back toward the campsite, concentrating on putting one green-splashed boot in front of the other. The color was ominously familiar. In fact, it was the same lime green she used for certain games at The Oaks. The exact same damned green.

13

MARNIE FELT a vague sense of surprise at how much time had passed. The long shadows of afternoon lay softy over the forest floor. She slapped at a mosquito, and Jared lit a cigarette. He smoked it in short, hard drags.

If her gaze hadn't been attracted by the way the spirals of white smoke held their shape in the humid air, she wouldn't have noticed a twinkle of silver in the underbrush. Her attention flared. There, again. A lightning bug flash of brilliance that rounded the straight trunk of an old chokecherry tree and was cut off from sight.

She hurtled after it.

"Marnie!" Jared's furious roar was lost in the loud rustle of leaves as the form ahead of her stumbled through a clump of creeper.

Fast, fast, fast, she told herself. *I have to be fast to catch the intruder and to keep ahead of Jared.* She knew his big-boned, cat-lazy grace meant that when he was angry, he would turn into an attacking lion.

Silver flashed again. Marnie knew the lake, the woods. The person ahead was running for the clearing where cars could be parked. She also knew a shortcut.

Without looking, she could tell Jared was chasing her, just as she was chasing the silver spark. He was perhaps ten yards to her rear. She could hear the steady thump of his booted feet and his disciplined panting.

Her sudden swerve sent her into the campsite. Without a pause, she leaped for the lowest branch of an oak and swung up to the rope bridge.

Cut off by the tangle of vines in front of him, Jared wasted only a syllable's worth of breath on a profanity. He had been trained for just this kind of job in another hot, overgrown portion of the world. The twenty years since then ceased to exist. Conditioning took over.

The soldier in him gave the bridge, the creepers, the surrounding area one comprehensive glance and decided on his course of action. He didn't have a chance in hell of catching up with her on that flimsy contraption of ropes strung between the trees. Nor was he convinced it would take their combined weights. So instead, he shrugged off the backpack, noted her direction and began to lope after her on the ground. Creepers forced him to veer time and again, which lost him precious seconds. After the first minute, her slender silhouette, weaving along the fragile, quivering rope bridge with the casual athletic confidence of a monkey, became lost among the leaves.

He'd seen a lot of monkeys in Vietnam. They'd howled and screamed and gibbered at the foolish, clothed primates on the ground, thinking themselves safe in trees that would be leafless after the helicopters came to spray Agent Orange. *Be safe, Marnie*, he prayed. *I love you. Don't catch whatever it is you're running after.*

Brambles tore at his clothing when he brushed too close to the creepers. Thorns from some damned berry—elderberry or blackberry—must be mixed in with the ivy and other vines, he realized. Marnie would know. He sure as hell didn't.

His breath was catching in his chest. A stitch twinged in his side. His heart pounded like a jackhammer. Too many cigarettes, he thought dispassionately. And...he was forty years old. Young enough for a good game of racquetball or a lengthy session of lovemaking, but those activities required aerobic spurts of energy. He could pace himself for them. They were also more fun than scrambling insanely through the woods. For a headlong chase, he needed clean lungs.

Damn. Forty years old.

The rippling of the ropes over his head began to slow, then came to a swaying halt. Marnie must have jumped off somewhere ahead.

Summoning up one more burst of speed, he zig-zagged through a thick stand of trees and stopped short, breathing hard. Half hidden in the brush, a pair of jeans-clad legs protruded, toe down. He recognized the length of smooth thigh and the slender sweep of the calves in the tight denim. Mist fogged his vision and time slowed down, measured by one, two thundering heartbeats. His voice yelled, "Marnie!" in protest or prayer. Then he was crashing toward her legs.

Marnie heard Jared and gave the ankles she was gripping a shake. "This guy isn't going to be very un-derstanding. Get out of here. Go back to The Oaks. Fast! Got it?"

A muffled voice answered. "Got it."

She fought her way out of the shrubs, hoping that the noise she made covered the rustling and snapping of twigs going in the opposite direction. Large hands clamped onto her hips and heaved her the last few inches.

"Thank you," she said breathlessly, although the hands hadn't been exactly gentle.

"Lost him?" Jared's rasping demand wasn't gentle, either.

"'Fraid so."

That was a lie, implied if not stated outright. She hoped her quarry had gotten away. *Oh, Kevin,* she thought. *Kevin, how could you think it would help The Oaks keep Frenchman's Lake to spike trees and plant paint-ball bombs?* The memory of the boy's white face and pleading—accusing?—eyes haunted her. Was Kevin's misery a result of having been caught? Or had he witnessed his favorite teacher in some decidedly unscholarly positions with her lover?

Marnie inspected Jared from under her lashes. Promptly, she shoved aside the troubling question of how long the teenager might have been spying from cover provided by the lush summer foliage. Right now she had a furious, frustrated and full-grown male to placate.

"I tackled him," she said cautiously, "but he wriggled away from me. I guess you were right about my karate skills."

As she expected, the grimness etched around Jared's mouth softened instantly. "Marnie..." Her humility hadn't completely defused his anger; she could hear the effort it took for him to hold back the harshness in his tone. But he considered her worth the try.

She could hardly breathe for the guilt she felt.

"You don't need to be embarrassed." His tone was husky. "I told you, fighting's different in a real combat situation. I'm not mad because he got away." He squeezed her shoulders and then yanked her close, rocking her. "But I'm not sure I'm going to forgive you for going after the bastard in the first place. I was scared for you, dammit. Scared right down to the bottom of my soul."

He was telling the unvarnished truth, she realized. The sharp scent of fear still clung to his body. A droplet of sweat that hadn't yet begun to dry trickled down his neck. She put out a tentative middle finger. The drop pooled at her touch.

"I never meant to alarm you."

"Well, you did." He didn't sound mollified. "Was it a man or woman?" he asked.

Marnie hated lying. She hedged. "Everything happened so fast...."

"And you're not half bad at the martial arts, which means the bastard was even better."

"Do you have to call the—the person 'bastard?'" she said irritably.

"It would seem to fit." He sighed and pushed his fingers through his hair. "Listen, honeybun, I know you want to believe everybody's a nice guy. That's sweet. You're sweet. But the fact of the matter is lots of people are Grade-A jackasses. You can't just dash off, chasing them on the assumption they won't fight back when you catch them doing something wrong. That person—" he used the word sardonically "—was the enemy. You're lucky all he wanted was to hightail it out of here, because otherwise you could have gotten hurt. Hurt bad."

Searching his implacable face for a speck of mercy, Marnie failed to find any. His mouth was grim. Metal would have been warmer than his eyes. Marnie licked her lips. There weren't any convenient choices here. Her most urgent duty was to get back to The Oaks and confront Kevin. If that was where he was going.

The soft curse she muttered was for Kevin, not Jared, but his brows snapped together. She decided to use his reaction to help her do what she had to do: get Jared to leave her alone. She would pick a quarrel with her lover. Her lover who was in no mood to extend understanding to an unhappy teenage boy. On the contrary, Jared would demand that the book be thrown at Kevin. Marnie couldn't have blamed him for his inflexibility if her life depended on it. The paint-ball bomb, harmless as it was in itself, had roused all of Jared's private demons. She wanted to shake Kevin herself for making Jared relive his worst nightmare.

But nothing would be worse for her student's shaky self-esteem. It was about time she stopped worrying about Frenchman's Lake, gave up indulging in the luxury of a love affair, and started putting her responsibilities first. Kevin was her student. He had to come before anything else.

Even Jared, at least for the present.

Whether or not they'd have a future after today, Marnie couldn't foresee. Oh, damn, damn, *damn*.

She drew in a deep gulp of the humid air. It caught in her lungs. For the first time in her life, she really wanted a cigarette. Something to hold on to, to fiddle with. Something to distract her senses from the horrible necessity to make Jared mad enough at her to go away.

"Could I have a smoke, please?" she asked.

He stared at her. His fingers dug into her shoulders again. "What?"

"A smoke. Please."

"Over my dead body." He said it like a vow.

Starting a fight was going to be easier than she'd imagined. She fixed him with a stare, hoping the misery churning in her stomach didn't show.

"May I ask just what makes you so sure you can tell me what habits I can and cannot acquire?" she asked with deadly sweetness.

"This."

He kissed her lips until they stung with the flavor of his passion. Marnie tried not to melt. A happy little murmur rose from her throat; she did her best to throttle it. "I'm not a brainless bimbo. Despite evidence to the contrary, you haven't turned me into a love slave," she declared, panting, when he released her from the kiss. "I can smoke if I want to."

"It's an oral habit," he explained, running a thumb over her lips. When they trembled open, he put the thumb inside and stroked her tongue until she sucked him lightly out of sheer instinct. "Obviously I'm going to have to keep your mouth busy until the fit passes." His protective rage was dying down. A wicked gleam lit his eyes. "Very, very busy."

Genuinely indignant over how easily he could manipulate her, Marnie batted his hand away from her lips. "I'm too old to be sucking a thumb," she said coldly.

"I can think of other things—"

"Forget them. Right now I want a cigarette."

"No."

"Whatever happened to 'life is too short to worry about prolonging it?'" She made it as much of a taunt as she could.

Jared looked at her with absolute seriousness. "I didn't mean *your* life."

Love washed over her. Shakily, she pushed the argument another notch. "Of course, Sarge. The great big man can do anything he feels like but his womenfolk are supposed to be prim and proper and not smoke and not chase eco-terrorists and always let the guy pay for everything."

"Jeez, how did we get back on that broken record?" he wondered aloud. "My tolerance for this crazy conversation is shrinking fast, Marnie. Look, I simply don't want you to pick up my bad habits. And I'm not too enthused about the idea of watching you throw up either. We're both already covered with green slime."

"For your information, I'm not a child!"

"Then stop acting like one."

She gasped, her own anger stirring. *Mistake*, she thought, but on her part as well as his. The lion in him was ready for battle. And she was deliberately baiting him. Still, he'd hit the button most likely to set her off. Too many doubts and tensions had underscored their relationship from the beginning, she realized.

In a hard, rasping voice, Jared continued, "You want respect, honeybun? I'll give it to you when you earn it. That means not recklessly endangering yourself."

"I can judge whether the risk is acceptable or not. These are my woods—"

"No, they're not. They belong to that damned school. I'm glad you're passionate and idealistic and expect the best to keep happening to you. But, hell, you go charging after somebody who's probably a terrorist and you expect applause. You won't get it from me."

"I haven't asked you for applause. I haven't asked you for anything—" Only she had. Quickly, Marnie shifted gears. "It's too bad you think I'm a—a grandstander."

"I didn't mean that. You're so young and whole-hearted you run full tilt into everything. I go into cardiac arrest worrying you're either going to get killed or have your heart broken."

It was hard to find material to be insulted over in what Jared was saying. Except for the crack about being childish. That one stung. Marnie clung to the hurt. She also forced herself to think about pushing his vulnerable button. If she wanted to strike back, all she had to do was look at his scars in a certain way.

She couldn't do it.

Not even for Kevin could she attack the part of Jared that had already been wounded so terribly. For one thing, he'd never forget. For another, she'd never be able to forgive herself. But mainly she just plain couldn't force her gaze to flick dismissively over the man she loved.

Marnie turned her head away, so he couldn't read the love she knew was in her expression. "I do want your respect, but you keep harping on age," she said. "You know, I think I'm a lot older than you are in all the ways that count. Talk about immaturity. When are you going to be ready for an adult relationship based on something real, like mutual trust?" She heard him suck in a breath to answer, and pushed herself to her feet. "Don't bother saying anything. You'll just get your army boots stuck in your mouth again."

She risked a quick glance. He sat there in the bushes, staring at her thoughtfully. Much too thoughtfully.

Turning on her heel, Marnie said sharply, "I'm getting out of here. I'll give you a ride as far as Bloomington. You should be able to hire a rental car there."

"Don't you think we should rinse off a bit first? This is kind of a conspicuous green."

She kept on walking. There hadn't been any sound of a car revving up; Kevin might still be around someplace, lurking. If there was one thing this trip had taught her, it was that getting near a body of water with Jared had certain consequences. Wonderful, delicious consequences that she wasn't about to risk with one of her students in the vicinity.

14

THE COLLEGE TOWN of Bloomington drowsed in the June sunlight. Suddenly Jared broke a silence that had been wracking Marnie's nerves since they'd left Frenchman's Lake campground. "Mind telling me why I have to scare up my own transportation?"

She should have realized he'd see through her argument. Marnie almost stripped the brake screeching the van to a halt in the parking lot of a car dealership.

"Because."

"That's not convincing."

"Tough." Her knuckles whitened around the wheel. "It's my van and I don't want you in it. I—I need time to consider."

"Gawd, you're a lousy liar."

She capitulated. Partway. "To think I was worried about damaging that ego of yours," she grumbled.

"Were you, honeybun?" His sprawl gave no indication he ever intended to get out of her front seat. "Luckily this very sweet, sexy blonde's been bolstering my ego like nobody's business the last few days. Want me to tell you about her? She's beautiful, but that's the least of her. Her feelings are worn on her sleeve. They're great big feelings. I think she loves the whole world. She just keeps giving. She's smart as a whip. And funny. I laugh when I'm with her."

Tears burned behind her eyelids. "You have to go, Jared."

"Why? What's going on? Why the mystery act?"

"What would you say if I told you I thought I'd found out who was setting booby traps at Frenchman's Lake?"

He frowned at her from under his brows. "I'd say give me my five minutes to tear the bastard limb from limb, and after that let's turn the pieces over to the authorities."

Her laughter was choked. "That's what I figured. Get out of the van, Jared."

Opening the door, he looked back at her. "You're sure about this."

"No. But I haven't got any choice."

"That's crazy. I don't want to leave you, and you don't want me to leave. Why should I rent some car for a long drive to Chicago all by myself when we can be together?"

"Because you follow rules. Your life didn't start to work until you made rules for yourself and stuck to them."

"I suppose so. Army, high school, college, career. What's that got to do with us?"

"Your rules tell you to punish whoever set the traps in the woods. But, you see, *my* life didn't come together until I escaped from rules. We have a basic disagreement here."

"So we can have a great time arguing about it on the way north."

"Damn it all, why couldn't you be a normal male and stay mad so I could kick you out with a good conscience? I've been bitchy and unreasonable and you should be overjoyed to see the last of me."

The creases in his forehead smoothed out, and he gave her his crooked grin. "It's reassuring to be right.

Seemed to me you were having a hard time finding excuses to tell me to leave."

"You're certainly driving me nuts right now." Even she could hear the catch of desperation in her voice. "Maybe I resented the way you beat me at karate. And then you had the nerve to lecture me about it. I could be getting even for that."

"Yeah, sure, honeybun. Well, if you want me to go, I'll go." He hoisted his bedroll and backpack from the space immediately behind his seat. "Are you heading straight back to The Oaks?"

She hesitated, then nodded.

"I'll call you tonight."

"All *right*," she said crossly. "Would you just beat it now, please?"

"In a minute."

He kissed her like a natural force ravaging the countryside . . . with the wet heat of a summer storm. Her mouth opened, accepting his tongue. She drank in the rough, sexy things he muttered against her lips. Marnie could no more have turned away from him than she could have resisted the dangerous excitement of a tornado.

By the time he lifted his head, she was kneading his upper arms and rubbing herself—with unpremeditated shamelessness, like a kitten—against every part of him she could reach.

"I'll leave now," he told her. "If you're sure you want me to go."

She had to order her fingers to pry themselves away from him. "Go." Her voice was steady.

"You got it."

He'd said he would call, so Marnie knew it was foolish—but her heart broke a little when he strode into the dealership without a backward glance.

Inside the air-conditioned showroom, a salesman lost his helpful air when Jared explained he wanted nothing more than a rental. Probably lucky the guy was willing to let him pay through the nose for a car at all, he thought during a visit to the men's washroom. Examining himself in the narrow mirror, he saw that this morning's sketchy shave with cold water had missed a few whiskers, and his lonely douse in the lake hadn't removed all the paint. His clothes were definitely the worse for wear. The scar across his face completed the derelict image.

He was amused rather than disturbed. Apparently, his gold card and sterling line of credit were enough to make him acceptable. When the clerk handed over the keys to a spanking-clean Camry, he realized he was thinking like a city dweller. There was always an explanation for eau de dirt and boots trailing bits of fern this close to the country. "Gone fishing?" the middle-aged man asked chattily.

Jared had a mental image of Marnie, waterborne and pliant, melting under his mouth.

"You could say that," he replied, and headed for the car.

Going toward Chicago, the sleek little import made better time than Marnie's ancient van ever could. The engine hummed, a sound quite unlike the chug that had been produced by the van's tired engine as it went over the same road the day before. Yesterday. The realization of how little time he and Marnie had actually spent together rocked him. They'd only been on this cockeyed adventure thirty-six hours. Hell, all in all, they'd only known each other five days.

Falling in love had been fast and hard. It might have taken forty years, he thought wryly, but once the right woman had put herself in his path, he hadn't wasted any time getting himself thoroughly—and as far as he was concerned, inextricably—involved in her life.

And now his taffy blonde was trying to uninvolve him. The almost frantic tactlessness she'd used to get him to leave her told its own story. He was fairly sure she would have been clear-eyed and gentle but firm had she really wanted to ease him out of her life. It was impossible to take seriously her spate of excuses for getting him out of the van. Almost as impossible as it was to believe cheerful, reckless Marnie was the type to cling to a grudge.

As the import ate up the miles, Jared's vague suspicion over Marnie's behavior gradually hardened into conviction. He had a crystal clear memory of his conversation with what's-his-name, the other teacher: *"The paint-ball war got a little out of hand."* And Marnie had been all too familiar with the slimy green paint.

She actually wasn't bad at self-defense. And yet the other person in the woods with them had gotten clean away.

Slim, lovely, athletic Marnie. So passionate and filled with ideals. So dedicated to the unconventional reformatory where she worked. So ready to empathize with the teenage travails of her students, having weathered some of her own.

His fist beat against his thigh. The land at Frenchman's Lake was a small parcel, privately owned. It wasn't the kind of old growth, government-controlled timberland that usually drew the attention of environmental radicals. Just a little, perfect stretch of forest surrounding a cool, deep lake. He had his own reasons to smile reminiscently when he thought of it.... God, yes, Marnie filling his senses, coming apart at the sweep of his tongue. But the kids at The Oaks had reasons to think fondly of the place, too. Not the same kind—as an adult, he supposed it was his duty to hope they didn't, anyway—but still, they would have reasons important to them.

And one of them had planted spikes and trip wires and a paint bomb.

Jared swore under his breath in time to the swishing of the tires. Marnie was nobody's dummy. She had to have reached the same conclusions he had reached. Hell, the infuriatingly optimistic woman had probably recognized the kid she'd let escape.

He growled out a few more four-letter words.

Speaking of spikes, his wood sprite was going to spit nails when he did the right thing—the only possible thing—and reported the damned mess along with his suspicions about it.

MARNIE PARKED the van in the spot reserved for her near her comfortable apartment at The Oaks. Right now a shower and a long nap sounded like heaven, but they would have to be postponed. There were more urgent matters to take care of.

First on the list was finding Kevin.

She'd managed to stay reasonably calm during the lonely drive. Of course, her hands had started to shake, so she'd had to grip the wheel painfully. The memory of Jared's harsh warning about rapists in back seats had inspired a permanent and unpleasant tingle between her shoulder blades. Which was ridiculous, because she'd never been afraid of random attacks. But once the fear began to stroke her nerve endings, goose bumps kept prickling over her skin, as if someone really were right behind her. And finally she'd pulled over to the gravel shoulder because unexpected tears just wouldn't stop coming. It was stupid and unproductive to feel so shattered. After all, she wasn't doing anything more than hiding a single fact from Jared.

If only he was a bit more flexible, a bit less likely to insist on some harsh punishment. Everybody had to accept that actions have consequences, and Kevin was due to learn that lesson in the very near future—but calling in the authorities would be the worst possible tactic to use against a boy like him.

Kevin was like a young tree with its growth too closely controlled by its gardener—the polar opposite of the trees in the forest. They were free to seek the sun. Kevin was a—a bonsai tree, she thought. Bent into an odd shape and trimmed within an inch of his life. The boy's father was one of those well-intentioned monsters who ought to have been given a parenting test before being allowed to reproduce. More pressure from authority wouldn't fix Kevin. It would crush him.

"Maybe you're reading too much into this," she murmured to herself, climbing out of the van. It could easily be that Kevin had merely followed her, first to Chicago, then back to Indiana and the lake. Boys in the throes of an adolescent crush had been known to do weirder things, go to far more obsessive lengths, and hadn't David claimed that Kevin might be infatuated with her?

The answer could even be simpler than that. It was possible that Kevin had returned to the lake for the same reason she had—to do some amateur snooping. In which case, she thought in frustration, she still didn't know who had spiked the place.

Standing outside the van with her fists balled lightly on her hips, she caught sight of a stocky figure in wide, colorful trousers and a school T-shirt. "Chad!"

He waited for her to run over to him. "Hi, Ms. Rainbrook," he said. Her scruffy appearance didn't even rate a grin from the teenager. Briefly, she wondered if she always looked unkempt to the kids, or if he was simply holding on to his all-important cool.

She dismissed the irrelevant thought. "Chad, have you seen Kevin?"

"Nah, Ms. Rainbrook. Not since breakfast. It was those weird scrambled eggs the cooks put green flecks in so we won't guess they're powdered. Gross."

"Okay." Her thoughts raced. If Kevin had been here at the school to eat, then he hadn't been in the southern part of the state watching Jared and her as they...

"You all right?" Chad was looking at her with confusion on his blunt features. "I mean, you seem kind of . . . worried and thoughtful. Not like usual."

"It's not a usual day," she replied. *There* was a heroic understatement. "If you happen to see him—"

Midsentence, she decided not to ask Chad to tell Kevin who was asking for him. Kevin must know that already, and the knowledge that an adult with good reason to be less than happy with him was searching for him might push the boy into further flight.

Shoving back the tendrils of hair snaking down onto her cheeks, she sighed. "Never mind. Just . . . be his friend, okay?"

He stepped back. "Wizard doesn't have any friends."

"Yes, he does," she contradicted him softly. "Me. But he needs a few more allies, Chad. Everybody needs somebody."

Damn, she longed for Jared. She wanted his seamed face and battle-worn body; his roughness, his gentleness; his wholly male impatience with what he liked to think of as her impracticality and the ready understanding that balanced it. His laughter. All the things that made him a perfect match for her own combination of street smarts and sometimes soft, sometimes lusty femininity—female qualities in her that his uninhibited maleness had forced her to acknowledge from the first. Only one essential ingredient was lacking in their relationship.

Jared wasn't her ally. Not in this. She'd asked for his advice, and he'd pushed himself into her adventure, making himself her lover at the same time. But underneath the financial daredevil who relished taking chances, Marnie had discovered a straightforward man who valued rules. Once he'd decided to follow them, they'd rewarded him beyond most people's dreams. The acts of entering the army, finishing his education and applying himself to long hours of hard work had given him a corner office and a luxurious boat. He had plenty of stress, yes, but also the opportunity to relieve that stress with the upscale sport of racquetball. Jared just wasn't built to decipher the despair, drama and wackiness of the kids who were oddball enough to end up at The Oaks. He'd told her he wasn't a mercenary, and he wasn't. Her lover was exactly the opposite—a straight-arrow soldier. Her good fortune.

Where was Kevin?

A search of his room revealed nothing except the fact that he was a fan of "Star Trek," with particular emphasis on the character of Deanna Troi.

"Well, that's normal, at any rate," she said under her breath. Posters of the Betazoid beauty overlapped on a wall and half of his dorm-supplied bookcase was taken up by rows of "Star Trek" videotapes. No doubt he'd transfer his enthusiasm to a real girl one of these days. Marnie felt buoyed. And relieved. If Kevin's taste ran to luscious brunettes, he'd hardly be fixated on a boobless blonde.

More worrisome were the beautifully handcrafted models of science fiction weaponry that littered the bed and floor. A few of them were comical; a phaser had obviously started out life as a woman's electric shaver, for example. Kevin hadn't been able to disguise the daisy pattern on one side of its vaguely egglike shape. But most of the stuff was downright scary: real-looking battle-axes and swords, as well as large rifles that would have been at home in Arnold Schwarzenegger's Christmas stocking.

She hefted each and every one of them. All were light and nonfunctional. What did the staff psychologist make of them, she wondered. At least when Kevin had put together a bomb, he'd only been armed with paint.

That's right, Marnie, she thought, *cling to the comfort available.* Reassuring herself that Kevin wasn't infatuated with her and that he wasn't about to blow somebody up for real, she circled the campus, stopping teachers to ask them to keep an eye out for Kevin. She checked the fields, the barns, the equipment sheds.

No mop-topped, undersize teenager with shy eyes anywhere. Marnie leaned against the hot fender of the old tractor he'd fixed. If he hadn't returned to The

Oaks, then his parents and the police would have to be informed. No way was Kevin equipped to cope as a runaway.

Admitting defeat, Marnie went to the administration building. Facing the music and calling in reinforcements would require the same confession.

"Headmaster," she said through an open door, "I need to speak to you."

"Ah, Marnie." Hank Corlin was short, balding and dumpy. He was also one of the most impressive educators Marnie had ever met. Not so many years before, he'd supplied her with the safe environment and carefully monitored challenges that had helped her grow past her adolescent rebellion. All through college, she'd known she never wanted to work for anyone else. His small, shrewd eyes weighed her as he gently cradled his phone. "I'm glad you've come to me. I just had a rather disturbing call from a man who says he's met you. A Jared Cain..."

15

SHE HAD KNOWN he would betray her.

Leaving Hank Corlin's office half an hour later, Marnie walked numbly in the direction of her van. Instinct guided her steps; in the wake of Jared's call to her boss, she was operating on some reserve of blood sugar and bone-deep dignity she hadn't been aware she possessed.

Hank had repeated what Jared had told him and asked if she wanted to deny any of it. "The guy says you went to him for advice about the trouble at the lake, he accompanied you to take a look and that a student was probably responsible."

No, Marnie didn't try to deny it.

"You're not fired, Marnie," Hank had said. "We both know you're a great teacher; an asset to the school. But your enthusiasm has to be balanced by the—well, call them the more reserved qualities we see in the rest of the teaching team. Going off half-cocked by yourself is dangerous for you and a rotten example to the students. So I'm suspending you for the rest of summer session. I'm sorry."

That had hurt, but she'd somehow held her eyes open despite the sting of tired tears. Hank's critique has also been just. "I want to help search for Kevin," she'd managed to say. Hank had already alerted the staff and called the police.

"Let's leave Kevin out of this. While you're on suspension—" he gave the word heavy emphasis "—I want you to give some thought to what the consequences would have been if you'd ended up in the hospital. Or the morgue. One, I'd have stayed awake nights for the rest of my life stewing about it, and that would have made me plenty mad because I take my sleep seriously. Two, your family would have sued; their insurance company would have insisted on it. But we can take comfort since, number three, once the parents of the students found out and withdrew all their kids, a lawsuit wouldn't have won any money anyway. The Oaks would be bankrupt."

Each point was like a needle poking nasty holes in her conscience. "You never talked to me like this when I was a pupil. You were always so—" she fell back on a word the kids would have used "—so *cool*."

Even as he scowled, a genuine-sounding laugh erupted from his chest. "Yeah, that's me, Joe Cool. Joe Groovy. Joe Neat. Joe Rad. The slang changes, but in some ways young people never do. Marnie, I used whatever worked to relate to you at the time. Geez, 'relate'—there's a word that dates me. Come on, Ms. Rainbrook. You're not a kid anymore. Playing Nancy Drew out in the woods is kid stuff."

Shock had chased the hurt, and turned her to ice. Under the layer of acceptance slid in the belated recognition that Jared hadn't told Hank what other games they'd been playing at Frenchman's Lake. The numbness made it impossible to feel gratitude, or indulge in wonder over Jared's motives, or...anything. This was actually worse than she'd feared. A student had disappeared.

Where was Kevin?

In a chill daze, Marnie left the building and briefly envisioned the places she ought to go. Back inside to her own office? There were personal things in her desk that ought to be cleared out to make room for her replacement. To her apartment, for the same reason? She couldn't stay here, that was for sure.

"Marnie?" It was David, jogging up through the twilight shadows, taking her arm in concern. "I heard about Kevin. Don't look so distraught. We'll find him."

There were a hundred things she ought to say to him—about Kevin, about Frenchman's Lake. Instead she whispered, "Oh, David, I've done something so stupid." She'd fallen in love. A tear trailed a wet path down her cheek.

"It's not that bad." But worry lines made furrows between his eyebrows.

Marnie pulled herself together. By a hair. Later she could fall apart over Jared's betrayal. At this moment, the only important thing had to be Kevin. "Where is he?" she demanded in frustration.

"We'll find him," David repeated. Behind him, far down the long, straight road that ran through the fields, rolled a black-and-white sedan. The police car grew in size as it approached until it passed them on its way to the administration building. A sleepy whoosh of humid air washed over them in its wake. The breeze was warm, Marnie knew, but she couldn't feel the heat. "You think he's here on the campus somewhere?" David continued.

"I told him to haul himself back here. And he said, 'Got it.' For what that's worth."

"Oh, if it was you doing the telling, I imagine he hopped to it."

She tugged on her braid, hard, to get herself to feel something. The pain was healthy and helped her think. "Even if Kevin did have a crush on me, David—and after seeing all those cheesecake posters in his room I find it hard to believe I compare—there were a few things he might have seen down at the lake that would have shocked him into a quick cure."

"Such as?"

"I wasn't there alone. A man was with me."

David's mouth dropped open. Then he shut it firmly. She could almost see him adding up the sexual equation. "The impatient Mr. Cain from the phone the other day?"

"Jared. Yes."

"I take it his impatience was rewarded?" There was neither blessing nor judgment in his calm, even tone. Suddenly Marnie was very glad she'd never pushed a relationship with him. Oh, Lord, she wanted Jared.

"Jared and I—" She stopped, not knowing how to describe what they were together. So she simply said again, softly, "Jared and I." Because there wasn't any time to spend on long explanations, she added, "He talked to Hank. He guessed it had to be one of our students setting the booby traps."

"Poor Marnie," David answered, interpreting her expression correctly. "Don't hate him too much for it. He must really have been between a rock and a hard place trying to make the right choice."

"I wish he'd chosen me." Then she shook her head at herself and faced an unpleasant fact. "That's childish."

"Human," he corrected her.

"Where is that little devil Kevin?" The fear in her voice was close to panic.

"Let's canvass the place one more time."

"Hank's suspended me. I don't think I'm welcome here. You'll get into trouble if you're seen with me."

David's reply was an arm around her shoulder. As if she hadn't spoken, he said, "Kevin doesn't have the right profile for a runaway. The probability is that he's on the grounds somewhere."

But what if he wasn't, Marnie thought.

More police cars arrived as the silvery blue of dusk deepened into crisp, ink black night. Fireflies flickered, and Marnie watched them without smiling. A secretary brought her the information that a "Jerry or Derick or somebody" was on the phone and refused to get off until Marnie Rainbrook talked to him. Would Ms. Rainbrook please do so in order to clear the phone line? The school needed as many lines as possible free because one of the students had run away....

Marnie went into the building, and studied the phone. A red light pulsed, indicating that a caller was at the other end of that line, holding. She picked up the receiver, pushed the hypnotically blinking button—and dumped the receiver into its holder.

INSTEAD OF GOING to his office or apartment, Jared had homed in on the boat. He knew why. Marnie had been on the yacht. She'd filled the cabin with her scent, curled up with him on the overstuffed sofa.

He tapped feathery white ashes into an ashtray and listened to a soothing recorded male voice tell him all about The Oaks. Apparently the school perceived callers on hold as a captive audience for an infomercial.

"At a rustic campus deep in the nation's heartland, teaching the old-time values of honesty and self-reliance..."

"I'm not in the mood, buddy," Jared said to the canned pitchman.

Marnie was honest; it was her emotional honesty that had blindsided him into loving her. So naturally, the one attempt she'd made to keep something from him had been laughably easy to see through. Would she want him back after what he'd done in response? God knew she was self-reliant—too much so.

The oily baritone cut off abruptly. "Marnie?" Jared asked sharply. "Are you—"

A final-sounding click interrupted him. He'd been hung up on.

Honest, self-reliant and evidently, mad at him.

Really mad this time.

Sighing, he stabbed out his cigarette and then pitched it into the ashtray. It was an action he'd performed twenty to thirty times a day for years. Somehow, this time, disposing of his cigarette seemed symbolic . . . of what, he wasn't quite sure.

Jared thought about that for a minute. Then he got ready to drive to Indiana.

AFTER DEALING WITH JARED, Marnie found a state trooper at her shoulder, asking questions about Kevin.

Was he a stable, well-adjusted child?

"No."

Did he have a fascination with weapons?

"Yes."

Had he ever said anything to indicate he might be afraid of disappointing his parents?

"Yes."

Was she sure Kevin was on the premises?

"No," she said.

Nevertheless, the police organized a line of volunteers to tramp through the corn; they all held hands in order to make sure no inch of the campus went unsearched. With a painful slam of her heart, Marnie realized the police suspected that Kevin might have built a working weapon and used it against himself.

"Oh, God," Marnie whispered. It was a prayer.

The young corn was more than head-high, with thousands of stalks and leaves and leafy shucks that were covered with short filaments that could prick, even slice, unprotected hands, legs and faces. It was punishing work. Accepting a flashlight from one of the scurrying organizers, she pushed it into a belt loop on her jeans so that it cast its light forward. Then she took her place on the line.

At the end of the difficult walk through the corn, Kevin still hadn't been found. The hands gripping hers let go and the students who'd been on either side of her rushed to a fold-out table covered with tall coffeemakers and piles of doughnuts. Marnie decided it was too much trouble to move and stayed where she was, vaguely aware that she was weaving a little.

"Here, have some tea." David thrust a disposable cup between her scratched palms. The thick liquid was dark and bitter. Marnie sipped it gratefully.

"I hope there's caffeine in it," she said.

"I hope there isn't. You're beat and you don't need something keeping you awake. Go get some rest."

"I have to—"

"Sleep. Frankly, you're not much use to anybody, including Kevin, nearly passing out on your feet. Get going."

Knowing he was right and hating it, Marnie slowly obeyed. Halfway to the apartment she remembered that her toothbrush and some other personal things were still in the van. Feeling fuzzy, as if her head were filled with cotton balls, she veered toward her parking space.

Opening the van's back door required a complicated series of fumblings. Finally it creaked open.

Scared dark eyes gleamed at her in the dim interior light.

Kevin was crouching amid the cracked plastic seats and tumbled camping gear. His hair flopped in lank strands around his smudged face, and he smelled of fear and overheated teenage boy. "Hi, Ms. Rainbrook," he said weakly.

Marnie sagged against the frame of the van. *Thank you, thank you, thank you.*

Strength flowed back into her. "Hey, there, bud," she answered, straightening. Her instinct was to grab the young devil and hold him, just hold him. Five days ago she would have. Then she'd have seen only good in a hug, but she understood that in this case her instinct would be wrong. Her voice and expression revealed nothing. "Folks have been looking for you. You're a valuable commodity around here, you know."

"I saw all the cop cars and stuff," he admitted, digging his knee into the shabby carpeting. He looked as if he wanted to burrow into the floor of the van and never come out.

"How long have you been in there?"

"Since you told me to come back to The Oaks," he said simply.

"Since—you mean I drove you all the way from Frenchman's Lake?" Marnie couldn't help it; great gusts of relieved laughter shook her. She had to lean against the van again.

Kevin smiled uncertainly. "I didn't have wheels of my own. A farmer gave me a ride in his truck first thing in the morning; that's how I got there."

She decided to let Hank Corlin handle the lecture about fourteen-year-olds hitchhiking. "Exactly when did you arrive?" she asked, and held her breath.

"Not till just before you caught me." Disgust colored his tone. "The farmer kept stopping at all these little towns. It took forever to go a hundred miles."

Marnie breathed again. The private activities she and Jared had engaged in had remained private, shared only with the birds and whispering trees. And maybe a few curious fish.

"Okay," she said, "now for the biggie. What were you doing AWOL at Frenchman's Lake, Kevin?"

"Well, *you* know, Ms. Rainbrook." He gave her a sudden, sunny smile. For once Kevin's face showed the grin of someone who is positive he's going to meet with approval. "I was fixing it so the property couldn't be traded away. So nobody would ever chop down the trees. It was a good thing to do, right?"

Easing her hip onto the van floor, Marnie felt old. "No, Kevin, it wasn't. It's not up to us to decide what to do with the campground. And there just aren't any circumstances that make it acceptable to plant booby traps that could hurt people. Ever."

Kevin's brief flash of happy self-confidence died. "But—but you want The Oaks to keep the camp just the way it is. I heard you talking about it. A lot! Frenchman's Lake and the environment and all that stuff. I did it for you! You're so beautiful, Ms. Rainbrook."

"Gee, Kev, I wish you hadn't said that." Expelling a heartfelt sigh, she wondered how to respond. It would be incredibly tactless to say thanks for ranking her up there with Deanna Troi. "Listen, those spikes are dangerous. You don't want to injure anybody, do you? Some logger who's just trying to make a living?"

A familiar defensiveness settled on Kevin's shoulders and became a chip Marnie didn't know how to help him shrug off. "I didn't do so much. There were only forty spikes." Marnie winced. She and Jared had found twenty-seven. Kevin continued, "All the bomb had in it was paint. That wouldn't hurt anyone." He seemed to think. "A'course, that was just the prototype. I was going to see how well it worked and put metal shavings in the next one."

Marnie swallowed against sickness. Those would have the same effect as shrapnel. The scars carved on Jared's face and his chest swam in front of her mind's eye.

"But, Kevin, can't you see the difference between saving the environment by picking up litter and spiking trees—"

He looked at her with dark, innocent eyes.

"No, of course you can't," she said gently. "That's it, I'm afraid. Come on, Al Capone. I'm turning you in."

16

"YOU'LL STAY HERE, of course," said Louisa.

Marnie expected to experience the familiar sensation of being both trapped and bored. Instead, an unaccustomed rush of affection surprised her. Her stepmother was still bossy, unimaginative and irritating in her designer-clad perfection. But she was also kind, if in a limited way, and only to select people. The rather dreadful lesson of Kevin had taught Marnie to value the good intentions of others—and to judge them with a dollop of common sense.

Looking around the sun-drenched solarium, Marnie discovered an appreciation for the bright colors Louisa had used in this one room. A love of color was something they had in common. Not much, but a start.

If she could camp out among the bromeliads and the orchids it wouldn't be so bad.

"I'm going to get my own place for the rest of the summer," she hedged. "Maybe permanently."

Louisa's beautifully plucked, brushed and penciled eyebrows rose. "I thought your old position would be yours again in September. You were suspended, not..." She obviously couldn't bring herself to say it.

"Fired," Marnie finished, with a rueful wrinkling of her nose. "Yeah. But I've been wondering if I could get a job in one of the Chicago schools. Then I'd be able to take psychology classes, perhaps intern with a social service agency. I need more knowledge and practical experience before I go back to The Oaks or someplace like it. The on-the-edge kids are still the ones I want to work with." She looked down at her hands. The scratches made by the corn were barely visible, but she couldn't forget them. "I'm not sure I can forgive myself for making the mistakes I did. With more training, maybe I'll make fewer."

Fewer mistakes with kids like Kevin, she thought. There weren't any classes in how to handle a man like Jared Cain.

There had never been a whisper of empathy between her and Louisa, but Marnie could have sworn the older woman read her yearning. "That broker person dropped by again," said Louisa.

Marnie's lower lip throbbed from the the hard bite she gave it. "Oh?"

"Yes, he keeps leaving messages with Ellen. Which she tells me you refuse to accept. That's very rude and cruel, Marnie. In fact, it's tacky. Never leave a man dangling helplessly."

"I can't picture Jared Cain dangling," Marnie said rebelliously. Seducing, driving crazy with lust and love, yes. Dangling or helpless, no.

"When your father and I met him, he didn't strike me as the kind of man who could be . . . led."

"Uh, no. You couldn't call him easily manipulated."

Although he *had* let her hurry him out of the campground and practically shove him out of her van. But he'd known she was up to something. Only hours later, he was going behind her back to the headmaster. Half-ashamedly, Marnie knew she hadn't trusted him, either. She should have told him that the interloper was Kevin. But . . .

Nothing had been straightforward since she'd met Jared.

Anger, guilt and self-pity weren't emotions she liked to have clouding her thoughts. Love was there, too, burning brightly like the sun behind all the unhappiness. Marnie wanted Jared. She just didn't feel fit to expose her messy emotions to his penetrating gaze. Jared, dangling? Funny, she was the one who felt as if not only the rug but the whole floor had been jerked out from under her feet. Being in control was obviously more important to her than she'd realized.

And she was decidedly out of control where Jared was concerned. Her jumbled feelings were proof of that. So was the unbelievably chancy move she'd made by giving herself to him as his lover after they'd known each other a scant few days. Love at first sight was a heck of a lot more trouble than she'd believed it was . . . when she'd been living in a merry fool's paradise, assuming it didn't exist.

Louisa was still talking. "According to Ellen, he says he even went out to The Oaks several times."

"What is this? You made it clear before that you didn't like him. Why lobby for him now?"

The look Louisa gave her was bland. Her stepmother's careful lack of expression could have been due to a desire to puzzle her. But since Louisa's personal philosophy was that the less a woman smiled or frowned, the fewer lines she'd develop, Marnie couldn't tell.

"Really, dear, aren't you listening? I simply consider it more ladylike to settle things with the poor man."

When her pensive stepdaughter just curled deeper into the chaise longue and wound lightly tanned arms around long, bare legs, Louisa sifted strategy. "Your father and I are going on a short vacation. To New Orleans."

"To visit your family?" Louisa had relatives in the deep South, Marnie knew. She grimaced. If the Midwest was swimming in heat and humidity this early in the summer, the gulf must be a steam bath. "Have a good time."

"So we'd be grateful if you could stay and watch the house for us. You know Ellen's not what she used to be. Actually," Louisa added with a sly glance at her face, "you could do me a little favor in regard to Ellen. If you were staying here."

Marnie rested her chin on her knees and narrowed her eyes. "Like what?"

"Things can't go on the way they have been, with glass breaking and problems with service. Either we let Ellen go—"

Biting back a hot protest, Marnie reminded herself of the disaster that had resulted the last time she'd tried to champion the housekeeper. "Or?" she asked carefully.

"Or we get her some help. Ellen would rather fancy being executive housekeeper, don't you think? I hate interviewing maids—it's so depressing and takes forever to find anyone suitable. But if you could fit it into your schedule . . ."

"That's blackmail," said Marnie, astounded.

A tiny smile quivered at the corners of Louisa's expertly tinted lips. "Well . . ."

"Oh, all right." Giving in with a hint of an answering smile, Marnie felt a kind of relief steal over her. It was nice to achieve the foundation of a friendship with her stepmother. Weird but nice. Certainly Louisa seemed to make Arthur happy.

Louisa chatted for a minute or two about Marnie's childhood friends who were in town. They could be found, she said, congregating at the country club or brunching after Sunday services at the "right" church. Calmly but with determination, Marnie shook her head.

Louisa nearly pouted. "We only want you to be happy."

"Thanks." Marnie flopped backward into the deep pillows of the chaise longue. "What I'm shooting for right now is how to live with myself. And I think I have to figure that out on my own."

"Your father quite likes that Jared Cain."

"Father likes a *commodities broker?*"

"He isn't too thrilled by the profession. But he was willing to give Jared the benefit of the doubt as soon as he met him."

Marnie blinked. "He was?"

"The Illinois Rainbrook Guaranty and Trust would hardly enjoy its current sound footing if its president couldn't judge a man's character. Of course, your father made some discreet inquiries after your visit. Compared to some of the sharks in the financial world, Cain and Marshall are quite respectable." Louisa picked at a tastefully pink fingernail, not meeting Marnie's gaze. "And Jared is a man, and you did bring him home. It's the first time you ever let us see someone you were interested in."

Marnie was still trying to make sense of her family's about-face. "You didn't care much for him, though."

"He's not young. However, you're a handful, darling, you always have been, and perhaps a very young husband wouldn't be right for you. It bothers me more that Jared Cain's a hard man. I thought—I still think—you'd be better off with someone—"

"Wussier."

"Gentler," Louisa corrected her. "You're an exceptionally strong woman. Strong women clash with strong men more often than they coexist with them comfortably."

"The man you chose isn't easily manipulated. Father's generous to a fault, but also stubborn and opinionated. He knows what he wants—and he's hell to live with when he doesn't get it."

A genuine smile, of the cat-who-swallowed-the-cream variety, warmed Louisa's pampered complexion. "He gets what he wants from me, never you worry," she said with a surprising giggle. "Don't keep your Jared dangling too long, darling."

LOUISA AND ARTHUR departed for their trip in a flurry of handsome leather luggage. It took less than a week to hire a young married woman who was thrilled to find a job that allowed her to keep her nearly brand-new baby with her while she worked.

"As long as you're sure it won't be a problem to set up a playpen in the kitchen," said Jerri Lee, looking back and forth from Marnie to Ellen.

Since Ellen had been cuddling the slightly damp three-month-old on her lap for the last half hour, Marnie was able to say with conviction, "No problem. When could you start?"

The air conditioning fluttered the skirt of the blue, impeccably tailored dress Louisa had told her would be appropriate for interviewing maids. Marnie smoothed it down. Even two weeks ago she would have worn something else—a bikini, a tutu, a grass skirt from Hawaii—just to prove her independence. She looked back on herself with tolerant amusement. What did it matter who suggested the dress, with its indefinable aura of moneyed authority? It had done its job; the several women who had answered her ad all seemed to assume she knew what she was doing. Jerri Lee had been the one who appeared most likely to fit into a household of older people and give the place a little brightness and sparkle.

The mother held out a plastic toy to her son. "I could begin in a week if you like." Ellen took the rattle and shook it enticingly.

The two younger women exchanged a smile. Marnie couldn't let Jerri Lee take the job without a warning. "It might be a good idea for you to get familiarized with the house before my parents come back from vacation. My stepmother's very particular."

If Jerri Lee sensed any potential for future trouble, she seemed cheerfully willing to deal with it as it came along.

I used to be like that, Marnie thought.

Pushing the thought away, she concentrated on working out the details of employment. Within a few minutes, they shook hands and Jerri Lee was hired. Foreseeing that it would be a long time before Ellen was ready to return the child to his mother, Marnie excused herself and left the kitchen. She had her own job applications to fill out.

The doorbell rang. She turned away from the solarium where she'd set up a desk for herself. Maybe the mail carrier was bringing a package. Louisa had promised to send a box of pralines from New Orleans.

She swung open the door. Instead of a uniformed postal service employee, Kevin stood there, scuffing his running shoes on the flagstones.

But Marnie wasn't focusing on the teenager, because behind him lounged Jared.

He was all bronze today. There were bronze highlights in his brown hair, and even his brown eyes seemed bronze. He looked indefinably healthier that he had the last time she'd seen him—tanned and fit. His shirt of deliberately faded russet-orange had an open collar that showed off his strong neck. The short-sleeved shirt also showed off all the muscles in his shoulders, arms and chest.

No fair, she thought. Despite the relaxed way he had his hands in his pants pockets, tension coiled in him. She could feel it reach out to her. It caused every muscle she had to tighten in response.

Marnie didn't have the vaguest idea what was going on. But the fact that Kevin and Jared were here, apparently as a team, had to mean something good. She hoped.

She should have known Jared wouldn't wait for her to paste her life back together before he came barging back into it. A heady feeling of anticipation drove her heart in uneven beats.

"Hi, Ms. Rainbrook," Kevin said with a sheepish grimace.

"Well, hello," Marnie answered, her gaze moving down to the boy. She folded her arms. "We check all guns and sharp objects at the door around here. Rule of the house."

He colored, but he also rolled his eyes in a comical, world-weary manner. Marnie figured her sally had done as well as could be expected.

"You need to be patted down?" she went on ruthlessly.

Her reward was Kevin's shy smile. "No guns or anything. Honest."

"Good." She stepped back so they could enter the cool hall.

"No sassy comments for me?" Jared murmured, slipping just an inch short of intimidatingly close as he passed her chest.

That shirt really was indecent. It was unbuttoned low enough to reveal a swatch of curling brown hair and, without clinging, the India-cotton fabric defined his strong pecs and lay flat across his stomach. The material looked soft and touchable. The shape of the body underneath drew her stare like a magnet.

"I love it when you look at me like that."

She swallowed, trying to moisten a suddenly dry throat. Kevin had moved into the middle of the hall, gawking at its Victorian splendor. She barely breathed her weak answer in case he was listening. "Like what?"

"Like you're never going to get tired of looking." He leaned closer. His husky voice was a tickling vibration in her ear. Distilled intimacy. "Like you just discovered sex."

That's how you look at me, and I love it, too. But she didn't say it aloud.

"Kevin!" Her croak came out embarrassingly loud. She cleared her thoat. "How about something to eat?"

When she took them into the kitchen, Jerri Lee had her shoes off and was puttering around, poking in cabinets while Ellen still dandled the baby. Called on for snacks, Ellen's new assistant had crackers and cheese, popcorn and soft drinks assembled in no time.

"We'll have to put you on the payroll starting today," Marnie promised.

"Think of it as a sample of my work," Jerri Lee laughed. Collecting her baby, she left.

Ellen looked after her approvingly. "That one's a hard worker. She'll do fine." The housekeeper got to her feet. "I have some grocery shopping to do. You all enjoy your chat." Marnie thought she saw Ellen drop a quick wink at Jared.

After she had gone, Kevin squared his thin shoulders. "Ms. Rainbrook, I guess I owe you an apology."

"Oh, Kevin."

He sneaked a glance at Jared, who nodded, and the teen continued with an air of martyrdom that said, I'm going to face up to this if it kills me. Marnie hid a smile. Kevin appeared to be wallowing in the drama of the moment.

"That stuff I did—well, it was really kid stuff, you know? There are better ways to draw attention to the problems of the environment. We can write letters to congressmen and file class action lawsuits against lumber companies and all kinds of things. Mr. Cain told me."

"Mr. Cain ought to know. He's a businessman, Kevin. He buys lumber," Marnie pointed out, not to tamper with the influence it appeared Jared was exerting, but fishing for information.

"Mr. Cain," said Jared, "likes trees living in the ground same as anybody. I don't support killing forests. And when you want to find out something about Mr. Cain, Ms. Rainbrook, you can come to the source. Me."

"You've both convinced me," she murmured.

"Do you think my grades are good enough for law school?"

Kevin's grades were abysmal. "You'll have some work ahead of you," she said tactfully.

He groaned. "Yeah. English and history, blah, blah, blah. World War I. 1918. We won." His shy look of triumph was marred by an afterthought. "Didn't we?"

Marnie's laughter mingled with a rasping chuckle from Jared. "Last time I checked, we did," she said. "Are you sure that's what you want to do?"

"I haven't quite made up my mind yet. Mr. Cain—" the glance he tossed at Jared was full of hero-worship "—Mr. Cain says to take my time and consider the options before I make a definite choice. He says I could get a degree in physics or astronomy like my dad wants, and then do *practical* things with it, like invent stuff to be used in outer space. He says Thomas Edison was just a grease monkey with a great imagination."

Marnie regarded Jared with wide eyes. "He does, huh? And how did you get to know the good ol' sarge?"

"Ask me, Marnie. I happened to go out to The Oaks the night somebody didn't take my phone call," said Jared dryly. "I seem to recall introducing myself to the headmaster, who was having quite a conversation with Kevin at the time. Naturally I didn't finger him, since I was never close enough to identify the master criminal of Frenchman's Lake."

Kevin giggled.

"But the paint bomb," said Marnie dazedly. "It must have reminded you of . . ." She hesitated, not wanting to say more and undo the good work Jared had done with Kevin.

"It did," Jared said. His glance didn't go anywhere near the boy, but Marnie could see him picking his words carefully. Love closed off her throat. *He cares,* she thought. *He cares for this misfit, this not very attractive kid.* "I was pretty upset for a while. But then I got to The Oaks and met this fiend and . . ." He shrugged. "It was hard to stay mad. I also recognized a fellow sufferer when I saw one," Jared went on, reaching for another cracker.

"Sufferer?" asked Marnie cautiously.

"Another hapless male who'd fallen hopelessly in love with you."

Marnie's warning look at Kevin was met with a blush. "It's okay, Ms. Rainbrook. Mr. Cain explained that you're too old for me. When I'm thirty, do you know how ancient you'll be?"

"No, and I can't say I want you to tell me, either." Relief began to relax her. Warm tingles spread all the way out to her fingertips and toes. She felt Jared watching her. Maybe the tingles weren't caused entirely by relief.

A silence stretched itself out into awkwardness. The kitchen was a tall room with too few windows. The last modernization had occurred in the 1930s, but the room's white-on-white surfaces and rounded corners were styles already being resurrected by designers. Stark white cabinets and linoleum—plain except for a pattern of black triangles—had an almost European look to them. Marnie studied a black triangle on the floor so she wouldn't give in to temptation and meet Jared's eyes. Jungle eyes, she thought, knowing eyes. They were all over her, warm and caressing.

Kevin began tearing his popcorn into little blobs instead of eating it. Marnie summoned an upbeat smile. "Why don't we try the solarium? Uh, sun room, Kevin. We can push the furniture out of the way and get down and dirty. Seems to me I promised you some special training, and it's air-conditioned. Mr. Cain can demonstrate karate. I'm not dressed for it."

"Great!"

Kevin said it at the same moment as Jared. The boy's tone was enthusiastic; the man's was resigned but good humored.

She led them to the door. Jared pointed the teenager in the correct direction, then put a large, insistent hand on the inside of Marnie's wrist. Her pulse knocked against his palm. Awareness sizzled in her bloodstream.

"What?" she asked, jumping nervously.

"I missed you," he told her. "I missed this." He kissed her, hard.

"No," she protested when his lips and tongue finally finished all the wonderful things they were doing.

"'No' stop, or 'no' don't stop?" he asked with interest.

"Jared, I—I'm not in such good shape right now. I blew something very major with my job. I'm suspended, did you know? I'll be looking for a job in Chicago next semester. My insensitivity and lack of foresight about Kevin could have injured him, and through him, others—and worse, I haven't been fair to you. In fact, I was monumentally *un*fair to you. You said I was lying when I told you I was confused, but it turned out I was telling the truth and didn't even know it. So you see . . ."

He was shaking his head. "What I see is a caring, competent woman who's too busy beating up on herself to notice I'm around. I don't like that, honeybun. I have all kinds of objections to it."

Marnie tried to regain control of the conversation. "How much time have you been spending with Kevin, anyway?"

"A couple of days altogether. It's a royal pain yanking those spikes out of all those trees, Ms. Rainbrook, ma'am."

"You went back to the lake?" She was astonished.

"I knew you were hurting," he said, "and so I imagined what you would do. I suggested to your headmaster that Kevin clean out the spikes and so forth. It's good to clean up your own messes. Any we missed will show up when the leaves fall off in autumn. The trees are deciduous, you know," he added, deadpan.

"You went back to the lake," she repeated.

"Yeah. Hank Corlin let me tag along with the group of teachers and students he sent out with Kevin. Nice bunch. I liked camping with you better, though. Swimming, too. Swimming with you is a very exciting experience." He lifted a blond curl out of his way with a gentle finger and ran his tongue around the shell of her ear. As the tip flicked inside, a solid, healthy jolt of desire ricocheted all the way through her system. It was like the other tender invasion of his tongue, that time at the lake.

"Will you stop?" she hissed, casting a harried glance over her shoulder to make sure Kevin was far away.

He sighed and lifted his head. "I guess we should go make sure the kid isn't making a bomb out of a lemonade can. He wants to make it right with you, Marnie."

"I'm the one who ought to be doing that," she muttered.

He murmured a curse as if it were an endearment. "You're a control freak, you know that? And you look so sweet . . . Let it go. Somebody else can do the fixing for once. It's Kevin's life, after all. He's the one who has to make it work. Admitting he was wrong is part of that. He can't be a man without growing up."

Jared was right. Again.

"What about us?"

Her voice was so soft he had to lean down until their faces were almost touching to hear it. He brushed her cheek with his lips. "What do you think?"

Putting her hands around his neck, she slid her fingers into the hair at his nape. How odd, she thought, that with Jared she could feel warm and marshmallow-soft and erotic—and exasperated—all at the same time. How odd and how comfortable. It was the exasperation that slipped into her tone now. "Since you're taking over my job for me and laying down the law, I assumed you'd already decided."

"Oh, no, honeybun," he said, gently detaching her hands from around his neck and swinging one of them in his own as he walked her toward the solarium. "No way. I'm waiting for you to make a decision about us. Let me know when you do."

17

THE BIG OLD HOUSE WAS QUIET.

Ellen was spending the night at her sister's.

"Kind of a sudden thing, isn't it?" Marnie had said pointedly a few hours before, watching the housekeeper pack a sensible flannel nightgown and a book with a lurid cover.

"Are you saying I can't take a night off and visit my only living blood relative?" Ellen hadn't seemed to be in any doubt as to the answer; she snapped her overnight case closed.

"Not at all. I'm saying I caught you winking at Jared Cain. You conspired with him so now you're blowing this joint." Marnie knew how Ellen loved hard-boiled detective mysteries. "Taking it on the lam. Skipping out. You don't want to listen to me yell. What did you do, call to tell him I was interviewing people today and he should come right over while you were both sure I'd be in the house?"

Ellen peered over her glasses. "Are you sorry I did?"

Marnie remembered Jared kissing her, Jared showing Kevin basic karate moves . . . Jared. "No," she mumbled.

Driving Kevin away in the BMW late in the afternoon, Jared had waved, but he hadn't said when he would be back. It was definitely *when* with Jared, not *if*. It always had been, Marnie thought. There was a kind of inevitability about the relationship that was both reassuring and frightening.

Scratch that, Ms. Rainbrook, ma'am—honeybun— she told herself. Not frightening. Scary as hell.

The only thing that would keep him from coming back was his determination that she come to him. *I'm waiting for you to make a decision about us.* It was wildly unfair. She was good at making decisions; she'd taught herself to be. Why the idiotic Victorian skittishness now?

Marnie was sprawled in the chaise longue, slowly sipping iced tea. A magazine lay opened but unread on the floor beside her. Sheets and a comforter had been kicked to the foot of her makeshift bed. For good measure, she kicked them some more.

The air conditioner labored away, moving the air so it swept softly over her skin. All the lights were off except the reading lamp, which curved over the head of the chaise longue. The tropical plants cast shadows that were long and still. They didn't quite sway, but looked as if they might at any moment. The growing things crowded the corners and glass walls of the solarium, their blossoms indistinct and mysterious in the dimness.

Marnie finished her drink, turned the light to its lowest setting and adjusted the backrest so she could lie back, but sleep didn't come.

Why did she keep retreating every time she and Jared seemed to be on the point of—of making a commitment? As far as that went, why had she always gravitated toward men who failed to stir her emotions, who never touched her deepest physical responses? There had never been anyone before Jared who turned loving a man into a dazzling, troubling, soul-altering experience.

She folded her arms over her chest and stared at the high glass ceiling. Dimly and far away, it reflected the light of the reading lamp and her own still figure. The slim body was nude. She'd told herself it was too hot even for the long T-shirt she normally slept in, but the truth was she was feeling hemmed in and overwhelmed, and the freedom of nudity helped. She wasn't really being daring. Plants covered the windows as completely as curtains. The woman in the reflection looked relaxed, carefree and ready for sleep.

Her eyelids weren't even getting heavy.

Irritated, she rolled onto her side and glared at the pale, spiky-petaled flower of a bromeliad. Maybe, the idea slid into her thoughts, just maybe it wasn't so easy to make a decision about Jared because whatever the outcome of their relationship, it was going to be important—it had been important from the first moment she'd met him. So much so that she was dithering and hesitating like a first-time bungee jumper.

Even though she'd already made the leap.

She loved him. Deeply, wholeheartedly, passionately. Her jitters were no more than belated complaints from her sense of caution, outraged because she hadn't consulted it before falling headlong in love.

Jared would say she didn't have a sense of caution, of course. And perhaps he was right about that, too. Love at first sight wasn't very sensible.

Whatever part of her it was that had taken one look at Jared and known he was the one had good taste, though. Back in the woods, she'd assumed he would always be driven by his past. But he was ready to face the future.

Was she?

With a sudden, happy smile, she got up and padded toward a phone on a low table. Calling her love in the middle of the night to tell him she was naked and hot and thinking of him wasn't sensible, either. But she was about to do it.

A scrape, like metal scratching against metal, shrieked softly through the glass room.

Marnie stopped and stood very still; her heart lurched. Vulnerability was being naked and exposed in an empty house.

A bump and thud followed the sound of someone breaking in. With a yearning look at the phone she didn't have time to use, Marnie dove behind a stand of bamboo bristling in a huge clay pot.

Dumb, she thought. *Dumb, dumb, dumb.* She should have been wearing pajamas. Unsexy ones. Instead of a glossy magazine, there ought to be a tire iron within easy reach. The world was full of dangers. Even the house she'd grown up in wasn't safe.

Marnie crouched, resting her forehead against the cool, gritty rim of the clay pot. Footsteps sounded quietly on the tiles.

A voice swore softly. The "Damn!" came out in a familiar rasp. "This is like reconnaissance in the jungle."

Her bones seemed to melt in reaction. She huddled against the clay pot, waiting for her heart to slow its frantic beating. It didn't. Where Jared was concerned, relief could be erotic. The annoyance she felt didn't change that basic response. But it did stiffen her spine and put a scowl on her face.

"Marnie?" Jared stared as she emerged from the rustling fronds. His lips twitched. In the semidarkness, his face was all planes and angles. The shadow cast by his heavy eyebrows hid his eyes. "Did I scare you?"

"You always scare me," she said coldly.

He watched as she strode defiantly to the heap of bedclothes. Her small breasts bobbed just the right degree to be alluring. The angry stride showed off her long legs. His breath didn't come normally until she'd whipped a sheet off the bed and wrapped it around herself toga-style. She secured it by twisting a piece of it around the section already draped over one shoulder.

"Did you jimmy a window?"

Jared nodded, thinking whoever had invented the toga knew what he, or she, was doing.

"Just another of your talents you honed in the army?"

"Uh-uh. One of my foster mothers had a mania about being in bed by ten. So I learned to be there for bed check—and not be there about five minutes later. Breaking out of the house meant I also had to be able to break back in."

"But why break in here? You could have knocked on the door."

The sheet was slipping. One exquisite breast peeked out. He wondered if she'd noticed. Since her mood seemed to be iffy, he decided not to mention it.

"I was being romantic and impetuous. Remember?"

"You mean—all that talk at dinner in Chicago?" She kicked the tail of her sheet out of the way and threw herself onto one of the deck chairs. "Sarge, I said a burglar turning out to be the love of a woman's life was *a* fantasy. Not *my* fantasy. It was just an example."

Resting a hip on one of the chair's broad armrests, he smiled down at her. "So you didn't like it?"

"My deodorant gave out. You're lucky my bladder didn't give out, too."

"You didn't like it at all?" he persisted, slipping a hand into her hair and massaging the nape of her neck.

She sighed pure feminine contentment, and after a moment she murmured, "I like the fact it was you. However, I'm really mad at you for making me fall in love with you at first sight."

"Didn't believe in it, huh?"

"Absolutely not."

"You need more romance in your life." He tugged at a corner of the sheet. It slid loose and the whole thing slithered to her waist.

"My life has been one adventure after another."

"That's not the same, honeybun. You rush in where angels would hoot with laughter, before they'd tread, but way down deep inside you've been starved for the fulfillment of a few healthy fantasies. You wanted a little affection, and what did you get? A sweaty grope from some underage boys with their brains in their pants. You reached for Greece and you got boarding school. You offered love, and a couple of guys who ought to be taken out and shot thought you meant nothing more than sex. The wonder is you never gave up on life. You still expect wonderful things from it. I want to give you a few."

The pupils of her eyes were very big in the almost-darkness. They made her look young. So young. "Jared, I chose to party and run away and toss away my virginity. I can't blame my mistakes on anybody else."

Controlling himself, he didn't look at or touch the pert breasts so temptingly near. Instead, he traced the line of her shoulder. "Sometimes you're so wise, it's spooky. Listen, God knows I'm not perfect. I'm too old and banged up for a sweet and generous woman. My ideals can be summed up in one word. You. You taught me to trust again. I juggle the stuff of life every day— real basic stuff like food and minerals, stuff everybody needs—but I've never put as much on the line as I'm doing right now." He slipped from the armrest and crouched so that their eyes were level. Paper crackled as he pulled two envelopes from his pocket. "Tickets for Greece. I thought you wouldn't mind if I bought and paid for them, as long as they're for . . . a honeymoon."

She licked her lips. The moisture gleamed. He waited, tension building in him until his hand flexed involuntarily and bent the tickets. It wasn't impossible for her to say no. She loved him, but maybe she loved her independence more. There were women as well as men these days who preferred affairs to marriage. . . .

Then, swiftly, decisively, her fingers swept the envelopes from his hand so they fell in her lap. Before his heart could plummet more than a story or two, she took both his hands and held them to her smooth breasts.

"I'd like to see Greece with you, Sarge," she said. "But Greece or no, I'd like to marry you even more."

DAWN GRADUALLY infiltrated the solarium, making everything seem alive and new. Jared had never seen anything as soft and fresh as Marnie's skin in the morning light.

"Go back to sleep," she said without opening her eyes.

"Can't," he answered, carefully propping himself on one elbow. There wasn't much room on the chaise longue. "I'm usually up and at work by now."

She peered at him through sleepy lids. "Am I marrying a workaholic?"

"Yeah," he admitted. "You don't have to worry, though. I've found this great new hobby." His fingers slid sensuously through the dark gold hair draped across her breasts.

Lifting her arms over her head, she began to stretch luxuriously, and then said, "Ouch."

His thumb stopped rolling her nipple. "Did I hurt you?"

"No, babe, of course not. I love all the ways you touch me. But there's a crick in my neck. I told you we should have moved to the chaise longue sooner."

"I wanted you then, at that very moment. The chair was almost big enough for both of us."

A blush flooded her cheeks. "I didn't say it wasn't worth it."

"Here, sit up. Let's see if I can rub the hurt away." Settling her against his chest, he kneaded her nape with slow strokes. "Honeybun, if I'd known it would bother your neck, I would have waited. It *was* only ten feet to the longue."

"It's just a little crick, Jared. And don't forget, I have a certificate in physical education. I can think of an exercise that would relax those muscles. If you're interested."

"Always," he assured her.

"Well, then . . ." Marnie rearranged her legs so they straddled his waist. "Golly," she said, her eyes widening. She glanced down between them. "You are interested."

"I don't think I could fool you about a thing like that," he said gravely.

"I don't think so, either," she agreed. Her hands roamed his chest, the scarred and unscarred sides. They slid down farther.

Jared drew in a quick breath. "I could make love to you all morning."

"Yes," she said dreamily, then her caressing hands faltered. "Oh, Sarge, Ellen's going to get back. We can't be doing this when she . . . What time is it?"

"Watch," he said, his voice hoarse. "My watch. In my shirt pocket, I think."

Marnie leaned over. Her hair fell over her face, and she had to use one of her hands to push the silky curtain out of the way so she could see. Jared stifled a groan as his disappointed flesh throbbed.

"The watch is sticking out—it's 5:15." She sat up and kissed his mouth, rubbing her soft cheek against his stubble. "We have time."

"All the time in the world," he seconded. "Come closer."

She snuggled up to him. "You know what's funny? There aren't any cigarettes in your pocket. Did they fall out?"

"No. You aren't close enough yet."

Her body arched as he drew intimate patterns across her bottom. "What do you mean?"

"I want you very, very close."

"Yes, but about the cigarettes . . ." Her eyes were a soft and dazed gray, but they looked straight into his.

He sighed. "I realized I was wrong."

"You?"

"Me. I gave 'em up a week ago. Life isn't too short to worry about prolonging it. It's too precious to waste. I want a very long life with you. Now, come here. I know we can figure out a way to get closer if we just have a little faith."

Her smile was sunshine. Her smile was faith in him.

A commodities broker and a schoolmarm. But as he urged her hips up and then down and her soft flesh held him as close as the two of them could be, he was a soldier of fortune, and she was his lady. They would show each other all the adventures loving could make possible. Now and forever.

A Note from Kelly Street

Heroes come in all sizes and shapes. In a romance novel, it's fun to read about a hero a shade over six feet, with all his hair and lots of muscles. My "soldier of fortune," Jared Cain, is a hero who looks the part (Jared would deny it, but *I* think he resembles Clint Eastwood).

His story was born in a true incident. My family and I were sitting on a sunny curb, enjoying a parade—it had bands, drill teams, marching soldiers. At the very end, segregated from the other groups, came the Vietnam vets.

Their faces broke my heart. In contrast to the smiles of the other participants, their expressions were angry, sullen, proud. Their combat clothes were—no word fits except *sloppy*. But their determination to be there, to be counted for their service in a war no one wants to remember, shone like a beacon. They were rebels, and they were heroes.

In *The Soldier of Fortune,* Jared Cain is a Vietnam vet who doesn't know he's a hero. He lets his lady, Marnie Rainbrook, drag him into a situation eerily akin to his army service, even though that service came to a distinctly unhappy conclusion. This time, two people love enough to create their own happy ending.

Heroes, like happy endings, are out there. We make them happen.

HARLEQUIN PRESENTS®

is

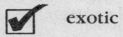 exotic

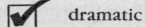 dramatic

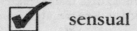 sensual

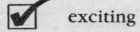 exciting

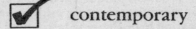 contemporary

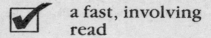 a fast, involving read

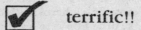 terrific!!

***Harlequin Presents—
passionate romances
around the world!***

HARLEQUIN ROMANCE®

is

 contemporary
and up-to-date

 heartwarming

 romantic

 exciting

 involving

 fresh and
delightful

 a short, satisfying
read

 wonderful!!

*Today's Harlequin
Romance—the traditional
choice!*